TARGET FOUR

(THE SPY GAME—BOOK 4)

JACK MARS

Jack Mars

Jack Mars is the USA Today bestselling author of the LUKE STONE thriller series, which includes seven books. He is also the author of the new FORGING OF LUKE STONE prequel series, comprising six books; of the AGENT ZERO spy thriller series, comprising twelve books; of the TROY STARK thriller series, comprising five books; and of the SPY GAME thriller series, comprising six books.

Jack loves to hear from you, so please feel free to visit www.Jackmarsauthor.com to join the email list, receive a free book, receive free giveaways, connect on Facebook and Twitter, and stay in touch!

BOOKS BY JACK MARS

THE SPY GAME
TARGET ONE (Book #1)
TARGET TWO (Book #2)
TARGET THREE (Book #3)
TARGET FOUR (Book #4)
TARGET FIVE (Book #5)
TARGET SIX (Book #6)

TROY STARK THRILLER SERIES
ROGUE FORCE (Book #1)
ROGUE COMMAND (Book #2)
ROGUE TARGET (Book #3)
ROGUE MISSION (Book #4)
ROGUE SHOT (Book #5)

LUKE STONE THRILLER SERIES
ANY MEANS NECESSARY (Book #1)
OATH OF OFFICE (Book #2)
SITUATION ROOM (Book #3)
OPPOSE ANY FOE (Book #4)
PRESIDENT ELECT (Book #5)
OUR SACRED HONOR (Book #6)
HOUSE DIVIDED (Book #7)

FORGING OF LUKE STONE PREQUEL SERIES
PRIMARY TARGET (Book #1)
PRIMARY COMMAND (Book #2)
PRIMARY THREAT (Book #3)
PRIMARY GLORY (Book #4)
PRIMARY VALOR (Book #5)
PRIMARY DUTY (Book #6)

AN AGENT ZERO SPY THRILLER SERIES
AGENT ZERO (Book #1)
TARGET ZERO (Book #2)
HUNTING ZERO (Book #3)
TRAPPING ZERO (Book #4)

For Patricia Allen,
who was always ready with a smile and laughter.

PROLOGUE

The eastern foothills of the Andes Mountains, in the Amazon jungle region of Peru
Noon

The three men and two women stumbled down the rough slope, where moss-covered rocks jutted out from the underbrush, darkly shaded by a jungle canopy. Here and there, where the rocks were too numerous and the bedrock too close to the surface for the soil to support trees, they came to an unshaded spot of searing heat and eyewatering brightness.

They didn't care. They didn't care that they gasped for breath in the heavy air, or that their clothing stuck to them with sweat. One limped from a sprained ankle, and didn't care. Another suffered from the mind-reeling fever of malaria, and didn't care.

All were hot, all were hungry, all were thirsty, all were at the very limits of exhaustion, and all had smiles on their faces.

The man in front, whose graying hair and mustache set him at an age apart from his younger, more robust colleagues, held something that might have explained their enthusiasm.

It was an idol, fully ten inches tall, of an Incan deity, and it was made of solid gold. The face was flat, with slits for eyes and a grimacing mouth. Framing the face was a fan-shaped headdress inset with lapis lazuli.

None of the five sweating, stumbling researchers needed to be told that it depicted Ayar Cachi, a god so cruel to his people that the other gods conspired to have him killed. According to one legend recorded by a Spanish Jesuit who came with the Conquistadores, Ayar Cachi had moved to a hiding place underground, where he caused earthquakes to torment the people above and wreck the temples of the gods who had betrayed him.

"Thirty years," the older man who clutched the idol gasped, the words coming out with an English accent that spoke of boarding

1

schools and Cambridge. "Thirty years of searching and I found it. I ... I can't believe it."

"Believe it, Professor Nasby," the woman shambling along at his side said with an American accent. "There's no doubt it's exactly what you've been hoping to find."

"Sir Nasby before long," one man corrected in the drawl of the American South. They all laughed, giddy with their discovery.

"Thank you," another man said, his Irish-accented words coming out as a labored whisper, for he was the one who suffered from malaria. He leaned heavily on another man's shoulder for support. "Thank you for bringing us on this. Even if I ... don't make it ... it was worth it."

"Nonsense, Professor Bridges," the Englishman said. "The first thing I'll do once we get back to camp is get on the shortwave and summon help. We'll get an airlift if we have to."

"We can sure pay for it!" the Southerner drawled.

Everyone laughed, even the usually staid Professor Nasby.

Their laughter covered the sound of rustling bushes behind them.

They continued stumbling down the slope. Their canteens had long since been drained, their food stores devoured, and they had nothing to run on except their enthusiasm and the promise of a meal and rest once they got to camp.

And after that, fame and riches.

More rustling in the thick green underbrush. None of them noticed. The jungle was thick with sounds—the constant buzzing of insects, the harsh call of tropical birds, the rustle of leaves as monkeys leapt from branch to branch high overhead, and the constant movement of ground creatures hidden by the thick foliage. The team stuck to a narrow path they had hacked out with machetes when they first arrived here a month before.

It was only when the rustling drew closer that the Southerner snapped his head around, his hand gripping the butt of the heavy revolver in the holster on his belt.

"What was that?" he whispered.

The others stopped and turned.

"I didn't hear anything," one of the women said.

"Probably nothing," Professor Nasby said, although he put a hand on his own revolver. "There's no one within a hundred miles. But keep your eyes open."

They continued down the path, more cautiously now, the forest feeling like it was crowding in on them on all sides.

2

The team had descended from the foothills into a little valley where the soil was deeper and thus the trees higher and the foliage more dense. No more was the canopy broken by open areas shining with the equatorial sun. Now the rainforest grew dark, a humid, claustrophobic place filled with a thousand sounds of unseen movement.

"The nearest people are miles away," Professor Nasby whispered, as if to reassure himself.

The archaeologist, famed around the world for his research into the Inca, would have liked to have hunkered down in a hidden spot in the jungle with his team, gun drawn, just to be on the safe side, but Bridges needed help and he needed it now. Besides, all of them needed food and water. Hiding out for an hour or so in this steaming hell would have made the strongest of them too weak to fight.

Assuming they had to fight. Nasby hadn't heard any suspicious sound for some time now.

Maybe a jaguar was stalking us for a while.

But jaguars don't make any sound.

Loggers? A native tribe?

Or nothing. We're all jumpy and Bridges may not be the only one of us who's feverish. After what we've seen, who could blame us for hearing things?

At last the camp came into sight, a level spot near a sluggish, muddy stream. Half a dozen tents stood in a rough circle around the blackened remains of a campfire. Between the branches of two nearby trees ran a length of copper wire. A coaxial cable ran from one end of this into the largest tent. The antenna for the shortwave transmitter—their only connection to the outside world other than a long day's hike followed by two days paddling downstream.

The team had cleared out the underbrush in a rough circle a hundred yards in diameter, far more than their half a dozen tents needed. Nasby, who had dealt with a number of nasty surprises in his years as an explorer, had insisted on cutting back the jungle far enough that a native couldn't shoot their bow or a jaguar sneak up on them, thinking of them as prey.

It wasn't far enough to dissuade someone with a high-powered rifle, however.

The first shot came when they were twenty yards into the clearing, still well away from the cluster of tents at its center.

It winged past Nasby's ear and took the Southerner in the throat.

Before the man even hit the ground, three more shots cracked the humid air, all from different directions. Nasby took one in the forearm. One of the female professors went down with a gut shot, and Bridges folded in on himself as a bullet pierced his heart.

Nasby bolted for the tents, crouching as he ran while more bullets hummed out of the jungle. He didn't bother drawing his pistol. They were too far away and hidden far enough into the underbrush that he could barely see their muzzle flashes, let alone their bodies.

His only chance was to get to his rifle before the shock of getting shot in the forearm wore off and he couldn't hold up his weapon.

More shots. None came close to him. He glanced back and saw all his crew down except for Irina Gonzalez, a professor at the University of New Mexico, who sat on the ground, her legs cut out from under her by a bullet, firing her pistol at the distant gunmen.

Professor Nasby kept running. The first edge of pain started coming now. He gritted his teeth and ignored it. Although sixty, he had spent his entire adult life in the mountains and jungles of South America and had become accustomed to pain and fear. This was not the first time he'd been seriously hurt and it was not the first time he had been shot at. True, then it had been the poison arrows of the Jivaro and not the lead slugs of some riflemen, but it made no difference. Death was death. He ran low and fast, his fatigue forgotten, blood pouring in a steady line of drips from his punctured forearm, the idol he had been carrying dropped and for the moment forgotten.

He had to get to that tent. He had to get to his gun and his radio.

A bullet kicked up earth and grass close to his right, and then again to his left. He kept running. Irina had stopped firing. He didn't look back at her. He knew what he would see.

To his amazement, he made the tent without getting shot again. Furiously he yanked down the zipper with his one good hand and dove inside, falling prone on the groundsheet. He rolled to the side, dodging a bullet that did not come, and grabbed his 30.06 rifle with the telescopic sight. In the jungle, it should have been kept in a gun case, but Professor Nasby never did so, preferring the meticulous task of cleaning it every night by the fire to keeping it in a case that would take a precious few seconds to open.

Nasby needed those seconds now.

He turned around, wincing as he accidentally put weight on his injured arm, and leveled his rifle out of the opening of the tent.

No movement from the tree line. Silence save for the relentless drone of insects, the witchlike screech of some tropical bird, and Professor Nasby's own panting breath.

He wiped the sweat from his brow and spared a glance at his forearm. The bullet hadn't shattered bone, only cut a deep furrow into the flesh. No problem if it didn't go septic. The first aid kit was in another tent. It might as well have been on the moon.

He had a more immediate problem. They knew where he was. They could come around behind his tent and sneak up on him unseen. No doubt they were already doing so.

But why not simply riddle the tent with bullets? He would be dead already.

They don't want to kill me, they want to capture me.

They want to know where the cave is.

Only one chance. He crawled over to the shortwave transceiver sitting on a crate of canned beans.

He flicked it on and the console came to life. From the speaker came the crackle of static. He tuned it to 7060 kHz, the emergency frequency in the Americas. It was kept clear by regular ham radio operators, and monitored by various government agencies and volunteers.

Hunching low, Nasby picked up the mic.

"Mayday. Mayday. This is the Anglo-American Amazon Archaeological Mission. We have come under attack. Repeat, we have come under attack. We are at our camp. The coordinates are …"

Soft footsteps beside his tent made Nasby turn around and fire through the canvas. A sharp cry told him he had scored a hit.

A huge Latino man with a shaved head, decked out in camouflage, leapt into view in front of the entrance to his tent. He shouted at the professor in Spanish.

"Drop your weapon or—"

Nasby swiveled and fired, but the sudden move sent a wave of pain up his arm. The man dodged to the left, and Nasby's shot went wild.

Surrender? Never! These must be antiquities thieves. He would never give up his discovery to them. He'd kill them all.

Before the professor could do anything more, a shot came through the canvas, piercing his temple and exiting from the other side of his skull.

Death was instantaneous.

CHAPTER ONE

Mexico City, that same day

Jacob Snow sat at the desk in the hotel room the Mexican army had given him and spoke to Tyler Wallace, his boss at the field station in Athens. The old African American veteran had just praised him for solving another mission, and was now proceeding to chew him out for running off behind his back to hunt pirates.

"You were supposed to be on vacation!" Wallace snapped.

"Terrorists don't take vacations."

"You think I don't know that? But if you don't get rest, you're no good to me. Look at you. You're injured, in mourning, and exhausted. You need to heal. The world can save itself for a few weeks. There are other operatives just as good as you, you know."

That last part wasn't entirely true, but Wallace was right. He did need a break.

Except that anytime he wasn't working, he felt lost.

"So what am I supposed to do?" Jacob asked.

"I don't know. Lounge on the beach. Drink margaritas. Join a mariachi band. I don't care, just get some relaxation."

"I could go back to monitoring chatter."

"You hated that job."

"I hate not working even more."

"Too bad. You're on vacation until further notice. That's an order. Don't make me come over there and beat you to death."

Jacob laughed. Wallace was one of the few people he knew who might actually have a chance of pulling that off.

"Look, I got to go," Wallace said. "Some more things are brewing I need to handle."

Jacob perked up. "What? What's brewing?"

"None of your damn business," Wallace growled. "Now start relaxing. *Now.*"

He shut off the connection.

Jacob Snow shook his head, lay down on his bed, let out a long breath, and tried to relax. He had saved the world. Again. He should be happy. Or at least feel a sense of righteous satisfaction. No, not happy. A good soldier died today. A Mexican corporal he had only met hours before had given his life for the greater good. But still, they had stopped a plot to set off a bioweapon. The bad guys had lost and the good guys had won. Mostly.

That should be enough. It usually was enough.

Not this time.

Jana Peters had been with him, like she had on his previous two missions. It looked like their fates had become intertwined, and he had finally decided to tell her the truth about her father and himself. He had broken half a dozen CIA rules to do so, but considering that it was her father and she had helped save the world from three different global disasters in as many months, he figured she deserved it.

But all it did was make her mad. She'd been enraged to learn Aaron Peters had become like a father to him while not spending enough time being a father to her.

Another reminder, among so many, that CIA agents had no business making close personal relationships. It wasn't fair to the other people.

Even superficial relationships weren't fair. Gabriella had been killed because of him. An innocent woman whose only crime was that she had been his part-time girlfriend.

He rubbed his eyes with his good hand. His other was still wrapped up thanks to an injury from a few weeks before that hadn't been given a chance to heal. God, how he'd messed up! Gabriella dead, and Jana most likely never speaking to him again.

OK, from now on don't get close to anybody. If you feel the itch, find a one-night stand in a bar or something. If they give you their number, delete it and never call them again. You're good at that.

Before Gabriella, he'd had many one-night stands. The thought of returning to that life made him even more depressed.

He lay looking at the ceiling. Wallace had given him a severe chewing out for running off without authorization, then heaps of praise for a job well done. Nice guy, Wallace. Been around the block enough to know that rules were guidelines, not laws. Wallace would patch it up with the folks upstairs. In the meantime, he had ordered, *ordered*, Jacob to take some time off.

So what would he do? Wander around Mexico City for a bit, he supposed. The food was damn good in this county, second only to Guatemala for Latin American cuisine. Maybe he could see a few museums and archaeological sites. Hanging out with Jana had given him more appreciation of the past.

But doing those things without her would only make him think of her.

Fine. He'd go to the coast and do some scuba diving.

Except the last time he'd been scuba diving, a group of pirates had nearly killed him and Jana had saved his life, so scuba diving would remind him of her too.

"Jesus Christ, I can't get her out of my head!" he shouted at the ceiling.

His phone buzzed. Not his public phone, but his CIA phone. That had been lost on his last mission but the field office had replaced it during his debriefing a few hours ago. It had been provided with the same number as the one that got destroyed. It was essential that a small list of trusted agents be able to contact him.

Jana had the number too. He fumbled for his phone on the bedside table, heart beating fast. Was it her? Maybe she wanted to apologize for her reaction. Maybe she wanted to meet. Visions of strolling through archaeological sites together danced through his head.

He looked at the screen. A text from an unknown number.

Unknown number? That wasn't supposed to happen. A glitch in the system?

He hesitated about opening the message. Could it be some sort of virus sent by a hostile agent? Or maybe a message from someone who the tech boys had forgotten to put in his caller ID? Or maybe it really was a glitch. If so, he needed to report it. Having reliable communications was essential in this business.

Jacob opened the text and stared at the three words and one number contained therein.

"Icarus Northfield Europa 313."

For at least a minute he did nothing but stare at the message, his mind at first a blank, then a whirl of questions and emotions, and then a heart-fluttering excitement that it meant one of two possibilities.

It was a cipher, a cipher known only to himself and one other person.

Aaron Peters, Jana's father.

But Aaron Peters was dead. He had blown himself up in Raqqa years ago in order to complete the mission of destroying an ISIS ammunition dump and saving Jacob. So who was sending this message? No way Aaron could be alive. Had Aaron given the cipher to someone else and not told him?

But he said he wouldn't do that.

Confusing, but even more confusing was the nature of the cipher.

"Icarus" was code for "Jana." Icarus, the son of the mythological Ancient Greek inventor Daedalus. Daedalus fashioned wings for himself and his son, but warned Icarus not to fly too close to the sun or the beeswax that held the feathers of his wings together would melt and the wings would fall apart. A warning against hubris. Icarus didn't listen and paid the price. Aaron had always worried his bright and ambitious daughter would overextend herself. Using a boy's name instead of a girl's was an extra level of code to make it harder for people to decipher.

"Northfield" was a term of distress. Back in the days when Jacob was healing from his Afghanistan psychosis, Aaron had told him a lot of stories. One was about how the James gang, led by Frank and Jesse James, got broken up. They had been running roughshod across half a dozen states, robbing stagecoaches and banks with impunity. Then in 1876, a fellow outlaw, Cole Younger, had the idea that they move away from their usual areas of operations to hit a bank all the way up in the sleepy little town of Northfield, Minnesota.

Frank and Jesse James teamed up with Cole Younger, two of his brothers, and a couple of other outlaws to rob what they thought would be an easy target.

Instead, the peaceful residents of Northfield had opened up a can of whoop-ass on them. As the gang emerged from the bank, fire erupted from every nearby doorway and window.

Two of the outlaws were gunned down in the street, while the rest were wounded multiple times and had to scatter into the surrounding forest and fields.

After an epic chase, Frank and Jesse James made it away to continue their lives of crime, at least for a little while. Cole Younger got captured and spent a long stretch in prison. When he got out, he went on a speaking tour titled "What Life Has Taught Me" about how crime doesn't pay.

Aaron made two lessons out of this tale. One: never underestimate your enemy. Two: everyone can change.

They had decided when they made up their personal cipher that "Northfield" would be a term of distress.

So Jana was in distress. More than that, she had been kidnapped. That's what "Europa" meant. In Greek mythology, Zeus transformed himself into a bull in order to abduct the princess Europa.

The number 313 was the code for Aaron Peters. It wasn't just a signature, but also carried the meaning that he wasn't in a position to help. It came from the year 313, when the Roman Emperor ended centuries of persecution by issuing the Edict of Milan, which decriminalized Christianity and allowed freedom of religion throughout the empire. Constantine, being dead, couldn't come to Jacob's aid, of course. That was the second meaning of that term.

So this message was saying Jana had been kidnapped and Aaron couldn't come to help.

Of course he can't come help, Jacob thought. *He's as dead as the Emperor Constantine.*

Or is he?

Yes, I saw the warehouse blow up. Hell, it took a couple of city blocks with it. No way he got out of that. So he must have given his code to someone else, someone he trusted. But this person can't come help me either, or even reveal their identity.

Jacob checked the number and found there wasn't one. Whoever had sent this had used blocking software, probably a sophisticated version too. He doubted the phone company could trace it, even with CIA help.

He called Jana, only to find her phone had been switched off.

"Damn it!"

Next he called Major Pedro Obregón of the Mexican Army, who had helped them on the mission they had just completed.

The major picked up on the second ring.

"Agent Snow, I was just about to call you. I was going to ask if you and your partner would like to come to dinner at my house tonight. That is, if you aren't too tired. You could come over tomorrow if you'd like to rest."

"I'm afraid there isn't time for that, Major. We might have a problem. I just got some anonymous intel that Jana might be in trouble, possibly kidnapped. Her phone is switched off."

"When did you last see her?"

"At the museum after the bomb squad took away the glass sphere containing the black fever. She, um, left. I think she was heading back to the hotel."

"Check her room. I will call the Teotihuacán archaeological site. There are cameras at all the intersections and all the gates. We can find out where she went."

"Great. Thanks."

* * *

Two hours later, Jacob and Major Obregón stood in Mexico City's central police station. Jana hadn't been in her room, and Major Obregón had worked with the archaeological site's security personnel and Mexico City's highway department to spot Jana leaving the site and trace her movements.

The footage showed the chaotic crowd outside the gate to the site.

"There," the major said, pointing to Jana.

Jacob was impressed. The major had only known her a few hours and picked her out of hundreds of faces.

They watched as Jana flagged down a taxi.

"Get a fix on that," Major Obregón told the techie sitting in front of the bank of video screens. He was a skinny guy whose police uniform looked two sizes too big on him.

The techie highlighted the taxi.

"Watch this," the major said. "It's a computer program that will automatically scan the make and model and color of the car, and the license plate if we can get it, and trace it through any other CCTV footage we have. We bought the program from a Chinese company. The same company that supplies their own government. If you're going to spy on the public, might as well buy from the experts, eh?"

"Fair enough."

Spying on the public wasn't exactly Jacob's idea of democracy and freedom, but considering Mexico's problems with the cartels, they didn't have the luxury to play softball.

God, she hasn't been kidnapped by a cartel, has she? No telling what they'd do to her.

No, I'm not thinking clearly. It's probably the same group that grabbed her coworker in Fez.

The screen switched to the view from another camera just down the road. The taxi passed right under it and the program logged the license plate.

They watched as the taxi passed through three different cameras, then got into a dead zone where there wasn't any coverage, before reappearing in a large town that was part of the sprawl of Mexico City. The taxi stopped by a group of schoolgirls. A young woman pushed through the crowd and got in the front seat of the taxi.

"That's strange," Major Obregón said.

"I'm thinking the taxi driver made an excuse to stop," Jacob said. "'Oh, look, there's my daughter. Can we give her a lift?' Common technique. Puts the target off guard. See how she's turning around to face Jana in the back? I can't see what she's doing, but I bet she's holding a gun on her."

The taxi drove off, the young woman still turned to face the back seat.

"That certainly seems correct," Major Obregón agreed.

Jacob's gut twisted into knots as the taxi got on the highway. The techie sped up the footage and they followed the vehicle across several cameras for several miles before it took an exit onto an access road the cameras didn't cover.

"Damn it!" Jacob shouted.

"Don't worry," the techie said. "This is what we call a fake blind spot. Criminals who pay attention to where the cameras are think they can hide here, but it's a dead end. The access road only leads to a few farms and to the next entrance to the highway. They have to come back onto the highway."

"What about those farms?"

"None are owned by the cartels."

Jacob decided not to mention that the cartels probably weren't behind this.

The taxi reappeared on the access ramp, but the timestamp was off. Two hours later.

"What were they doing during that time?" Major Obregón wondered.

"Freeze on a closeup," Jacob said.

The techie did as he asked and they stared at the driver.

"That's not the same guy," Jacob said. "They switched drivers. I bet they put her in a different car. They knew about your trap."

"We'll find them," the techie said, sounding irritated that someone had one-upped him.

He scrolled back in time to a few minutes after the taxi had gone off the highway. They waited, watching every vehicle that came on. A beat-up pickup truck. A convertible. Then three more cars.

"Follow the one with tinted windows," Jacob said.

The techie was already on it, selecting it for the monitoring software to follow.

He followed it for a couple of miles as it passed different cameras and got in the fast lane.

"It's them," Jacob said.

"Lots of cars have tinted windows," Major Obregón said.

"Yeah, but see how he merges? Extra careful. And even in the fast lane he's keeping to the speed limit. He doesn't want to attract attention. Your usual Mexican driver cuts people off and speeds like his house is on fire."

"Thanks," Major Obregón grumbled.

The techie shrugged his skinny shoulders. "He's right, though."

The techie sped up the program and followed the four-door with tinted windows for several miles until it got off on an access road and they lost it. The program picked up the vehicle again in a built-up area.

"A town called Zempoala," the techie said. "They're going right through it. This is the last camera on the edge of town. They are going into the country again. Oh!"

Two different red indicators came on.

"What do those mean?" Jacob asked.

The techie pointed at the screen. "This one says the vehicle doesn't appear on any more cameras, and this one says the disappearance is close to a suspicious property."

"What suspicious property?"

He typed for a moment.

"This one."

He brought up the file. Major Obregón swore. Jacob took a little longer to read the Spanish, and then he swore too.

"I'll call for reinforcements," the major said.

Jacob nodded. Reinforcements sounded like a good idea.

CHAPTER TWO

Jana Peters paced around the tiny room, looking for a way out, looking for a weapon. She found neither.

Except a little black spot on the upper corner of the ceiling where two walls met. She peered at it and realized it was a tiny camera. They would watch her, even when she used the toilet. She gave the camera the finger, vowed to break it somehow when she needed to pee, and continued to pace back and forth across her cell.

Damn that man. Just when she thought she could walk out of Jacob's life forever, his life gets her captured.

Jana bided her time. Her kidnappers had driven on a highway for several miles before pulling off on an access road where she was transferred to a sedan with tinted windows. She was blindfolded, handcuffed, and told to keep quiet.

Jana had tried to follow the car's turns to get a general idea of where they were taking her, but it proved too complicated. All she figured out was that they had followed the access road for a time before returning to the highway and went in the same direction as before. She had no idea of their speed, but they kept on the highway for about half an hour before exiting. Then they had passed through a town. The car had stopped and started as if at streetlights and busy traffic and she could hear other vehicles, music, and the occasional voice all around her. The kidnappers had remained silent.

Then they had sped up for another fifteen minutes or so, obviously having left the town behind, before having to slow down to go along a gravel road. After another ten minutes or so, they had stopped, she heard the sound of a gate opening, and they had driven through.

She had been taken out of the car and led across a broad section of grass, the sound of movement and low voices all around her, and then inside a building. After a few turns and passing through three doors, her captors had taken off her blindfold and her handcuffs.

They had brought her to a small windowless room equipped with a cot, a toilet, and a sink. The taxi driver and the young woman who had posed as the driver's daughter stood in front of her, aiming pistols at her chest. A large man she didn't recognize stood in the hallway, wearing camouflage and gripping an M16.

The taxi driver spoke.

"You are being held here until we extract certain information from another person. This person cares about you, or at least he says he does. If he cooperates, you will be set free. If he lies or tries to escape, or refuses to cooperate, you will lose a finger. We will send him that finger. If he continues to defy us, you will be killed."

"Who are you?" Jana demanded.

The taxi driver smiled. "Surely you don't expect me to answer that question."

"What information do you want, and who is this person you're questioning? Jacob? Have you captured him too?"

"Stay here and don't cause trouble. There's a guard outside the door at all times. You must be exhausted after your ordeal. We'll bring lunch in an hour."

The taxi driver and the young woman left the room. The sentry remained in position, staring at Jana as the door shut and a heavy bolt slammed into place with a bang.

And she was alone.

Jana continued to pace.

At least she was still alive, unlike Jacob's girlfriend. That poor woman, who didn't even know what he did for a living, had been killed in a trap laid for him.

Jana thought of her, and the Mexican corporal who died earlier today.

That man causes collateral damage wherever he goes. If I get out of here, I'm getting as far away from Jacob as possible.

The pacing continued, back and forth, back and forth, until boredom and exhaustion pulled her to the bed, where she lay down and, despite her situation, she drifted off to sleep.

A smart soldier gets his sleep when he can, her father used to say. *A soldier never knows when he'll get another chance.*

* * *

Jana wasn't sure how long she slept before a deep thud woke her up. It felt like a long time, because her head was muzzy and her body heavy. Her half-conscious mind had the feeling that it wasn't the first thud she had heard, that it had taken several to pull her from a deep slumber.

Nor was it the last. Another thud reverberated through the building, louder this time, deeper, strong enough for her to feel the vibration.

She stood, fully awake now, and moved toward the door.

Just as she did, it swung open.

The sentry stood there, M16 leveled.

"Come out of there!" he ordered, his voice tinged with a note of panic.

Watch a frightened man carefully, her father used to say. *He's dangerous because his fear will make him do unpredictable things. He's also vulnerable because his fear will cause him to make mistakes.*

"What's going on?" Jana asked.

They spoke in Spanish. The man was Mexican and Jana was fluent.

"Shut up and get out of there. We don't have time."

No time to put handcuffs on me?

She came out with her hands up.

"Walk down the hallway. No sudden moves."

Jana walked slowly down the corridor, the guard following close behind. There were no windows in the concrete walls, and the heavy steel doors to either side were shut. Even so, she heard the sound of firing outside.

A louder explosion somewhere behind them rocked the corridor. Jana turned and saw dust billowing from below a doorway at the far end of the hall.

Her guard had turned too, realized his mistake, and turned back to her.

Too late. Jana lashed out with a kick to the knee that made him cry out and stagger, then followed up with her forked fingers jabbing both his eyes.

He cried out again and smacked her with the M16. Jana had hoped her special treatment would have made him drop it. Instead, it had just angered this man mountain.

She hit the wall hard, then found herself pinned as the half-blinded guard pressed her against the concrete with the hard metal of the assault rifle.

Her arms were pressed to her sides, but she could still bend them.

Enough to pull the pistol from his belt, flick off the safety, and, just as he realized what was happening and backed off, shoot him in the gut.

16

He doubled over with a groan before making a final effort to raise his gun.

She took him out with a shot to the head.

After letting out a little shudder, Jana scooped up his M16 and grabbed an extra magazine from his vest, stuffing it into her pocket. She tucked the pistol into the waistband of her pocket.

Then she wavered, the hallway rocking back and forth for a moment as she felt sick.

It was him or me.

The truth of that statement helped only a little. Since being torn out of her old life by Jacob, she had killed many people. They were all bad, all killed in self-defense or to defend the world, but the killing didn't come easy.

Real soldiers don't brag about their kills, her father used to say. *Real soldiers regret every person they put down, even if it's the right thing to do. It's the heaviest burden we have to bear.*

Jana tried to absorb that as she ran down the hallway in the direction of the explosion. That's where the assaulting force was advancing. Wherever the guard was taking her was still held by the enemy.

Maybe not for long. Despite the closed doors and thick concrete walls, the volume and tempo of gunfire were increasing.

There was a serious battle going on out there. Jacob had brought along the cavalry.

Because it had to be Jacob. As annoying and soulless as that guy was, he was the best. There was no better agent in the world since her father got killed in action.

As she got halfway down the hall, the door she was headed for burst open.

Two men in Mexican army uniforms, looking inhuman with their Kevlar and gas masks, rushed through the doorway, smoke curling around them. One leveled an assault rifle at her, the other a grenade launcher.

"Wait! It's me, Jana Peters!" she shouted in Spanish.

The man with the grenade launcher tore his mask off.

It was Jacob.

"Why are you speaking Spanish?" he asked with a grin. "Don't you know I speak English?"

"Jacob! I—"

His face went serious. "Duck!"

She hit the ground, turning to face whatever threat had appeared behind her.

It was a slim Anglo man who had emerged from one of the side rooms, gripping a pistol.

The Mexican soldier took him out with a single shot.

"The guard I killed was taking me in that direction," she said, gesturing.

"We need to extract you. The army boys will clear this up."

They spoke in Spanish for the benefit of the soldier. They both lived such international lives that such things had become second nature.

"No, we need to move on, figure out who captured me and why."

"The Mexicans think this is a people-smuggling base, at least they did until we faced heavy guns and found no smuggled people."

"We'll find out the truth if we can take a prisoner."

A couple more soldiers joined them through the smoke, and they worked down the hallway, clearing each side room. Most were storage, a couple were empty, and two were unoccupied cells like the one Jana had been put in.

"How did you find me?" Jana asked as they continued clearing the building.

"Traced the car by camera and then figured out which vehicle they transferred you to. Once they went out of sight of CCTV close to a potential criminal property, we knew we had the right one," Jacob said.

"Thank you."

"Don't mention it. Let's do this."

They were at the final door. A soldier hurried up, carrying a spare gas mask. He gave it to Jana, who put it on, and then one of the soldiers opened the door and chucked a tear gas grenade through.

No response. With Jacob leading, they rushed through the door one by one, guns leveled.

They found a stairway. Jacob used the grenade launcher to shoot a flashbang up the stairs. When it burst, he followed it with more tear gas and they rushed upstairs to an open doorway. Jacob launched another tear gas grenade through it.

They rushed the door and entered a large office filled with computers and radio equipment. All the computer screens were blank. Jana suspected they had been wiped.

Wiped by the man who staggered coughing in the center of the room.

His bleary eyes focused on the soldiers pouring through the doorway.

"Hands up! Hands up or we'll shoot," one of the soldiers ordered.

He blinked, coughed, and put a hand up.

Only one. In a Nazi salute.

"*Sieg Heil!*"

Then he clenched his teeth on something inside his mouth, choked, leaned against a desk for a moment, then slowly slid to the floor.

Jana hurried over to him and opened his mouth. The shattered remains of a glass ampoule were in his mouth.

"Cyanide," she said. "He killed himself."

"Why the Hitler salute?" one of the soldiers asked. He had on a major's stripes and Jana thought the muffled voice sounded like Major Obregón's. "Hitler wanted to kill everyone who wasn't white, and this man's Mexican. Look at his face. He's got a lot of native blood too. It doesn't make any sense."

"Nazism holds a strange fascination for a lot of people," Jana said. "In the Middle East, I've met a lot of people who idolize Hitler, even though he would have looked down on them as subhuman."

"Why would Nazis want to kidnap you?" the major asked. "And why would they have a base outside of Mexico City?"

Jana shook her head. She didn't have the answers to those questions, or to the many other questions crowding her mind.

She didn't have the answers to anything.

But she had the feeling that if she wanted to live, she had better find out.

CHAPTER THREE

Jacob Snow was feeling seriously confused. They had cleared the base. Every one of the twenty people there had either gone down fighting, or taken cyanide to avoid capture. They had no one to question about the group's identity and motives.

Whoever they were, they were committed.

And dangerous. Despite their better armor and equipment, the Mexican army had taken three casualties. One was in emergency care and probably wouldn't make it.

More decent people losing their lives in the shadow war between good and evil.

But what evil? Who were these people?

They found few clues in the base. Most of the bodies appeared to be Mexican nationals with a couple of Anglos mixed in. The computers had all been wiped, and they had found no written correspondence.

They had also found no Nazi paraphernalia. Jacob was thinking that the guy yelling *"Sieg Heil"* before dying had been a false flag, something to divert attention from the group's real motives. A gesture like that was designed to shock so much as to make the viewer lose perspective. Neo-Nazis tended to have lots of swastikas and pictures of Hitler and junk like that. They had found none.

Now, after a couple of hours searching, they were in the back of a Humvee returning to the hotel. Jana seemed fine.

"So your captors said nothing?"

"No," Jana grumbled, staring out the window, "only that they were going to threaten my life if someone didn't talk. Whoever it was would get one of my fingers delivered to them if they didn't cooperate, and I'd be killed if they continued to resist."

Jana said this with remarkable calm. She really was her father's daughter.

"But I didn't get any notice of your abduction. So who could they have meant?"

"Maybe they didn't have time to contact you. You got to me pretty quick."

Jacob gave a little bow. "Always at your service, madam."

Jana shot him an angry look. "Not anymore. I'm getting as far away from you as possible."

"What? Why?"

"Because you're constant trouble. Ever since you came uninvited into my life you've caused me nothing but headaches and grief. It's a miracle I'm still alive."

Jacob grimaced, thinking of Gabriella.

Jana went on. "I want my life back. I don't want to be running around doing this crap. For Christ's sake, Jacob, I got abducted less than a month after a friend of mine, an innocent civilian who had no idea what was going on."

An innocent civilian. Yeah, lots of those had suffered because of his line of work. But a lot more would have suffered if he didn't do what he did.

Shouldn't she, of all people, understand that?

Before he could think of something to say, she continued.

"We're going back to the hotel, I'm going to take a shower, eat a big meal, drink half a dozen margaritas by the pool, and sleep for the next forty-eight hours. Then I'm flying home. No missions, no gunfights, and no more blood on my hands. You got that?"

Jacob only nodded, too sad to speak.

* * *

"You did good, Agent Snow."

Tyler Wallace was on a secured video call with him. The grizzled old African American veteran looked concerned. Then again, he always looked concerned. After so many years in the military and the CIA, he couldn't have had a single illusion left in his brain.

"Thank you. Any indication yet who these jokers were who abducted Jana?"

"None so far. Mexican intel thought they were people smugglers because they had noticed an efficient organization with guns who had no known ties to the narco cartels. A reasonable assumption on their part, but obviously incorrect given what we saw. We haven't picked up any related chatter. Whoever they are, they know how to operate under the radar."

Jacob nodded. While the CIA and allied organizations at home and abroad did a good job monitoring most communications, the sheer vastness of online, phone, and radio comms made it impossible to

21

analyze it all. If a group was careful, speaking in code and only when necessary, and changing their means of communication on a regular basis, it would be difficult to tease out any information about them.

"We'll keep looking, of course," Wallace said. "From what we've determined so far, and from what the Mexicans have shared with us, there's no indication they were involved with the pirates who tried to release that old bioweapon, or with the Nazis who attacked the Dome of the Rock."

"I didn't get that impression, either."

"We'll tell you more as we know it."

"And Gabriella's murder?"

Wallace looked uncomfortable. "We'll tell you more as we know it."

Jacob cursed under his breath. Whoever killed his girlfriend while trying for him had been good, really good. They hadn't left a trace.

The kidnappers who took Jana had been almost as good. Was there a connection?

Wallace went on.

"We're putting all available resources on it. We're not stretched as thin as the Latin American bureaus. Things are heating up in Venezuela. There's a ninety percent chance of a revolution or at least mass social unrest in the coming two weeks. It's the same situation in Peru. All our field agents are busy monitoring the situation, along with dealing with the narco threat and terrorist groups trying to establish bases in Latin America. Which brings me to a question ..." Tyler Wallace shifted uncomfortably. "... are you feeling fit for duty, Agent Snow?"

Jacob blinked. Just a couple of weeks ago, after the bombing, Wallace had taken him off duty and ordered him to rest. Just a couple of hours ago, he had chewed him out for not following those orders. Now he was asking if he was fit for duty?

"Well, I'm a bit beat up and my gun hand is still sprained, but you wouldn't be asking if you didn't need me. What's up?"

"An archaeological team has gone missing in the Peruvian Amazon. It was led by Professor Carstairs Nasby of the University of Cambridge, along with several other researchers. We don't know their names but at least two of them are American. The field office in Mexico City has more details. The team had been in the Amazon for some time when Nasby radioed out a distress signal. Gunshots were heard in the background before the transmission ceased. We need someone to go down there and assess the situation."

"If there were gunshots, then they're probably dead."

"Quite likely. There have been no ransom demands. But if they were killed, who did it? Narcos? Shining Path guerrillas? Local natives? Even illegal loggers have been known to shoot people who interrupt their operations. We need to find the guilty party and extract any survivors. I wouldn't be asking if we weren't stretched to the limit, and I entirely understand if you say no. By all rights, you should be recuperating on a beach for the next month."

Jacob thought about that. A month on a beach sounded nice most of the time. But a month of inactivity would be a month of thinking about Gabriella. A month of torture.

"I'd rather pursue Gabriella's murderers."

"As I explained to you, several times, you don't have sufficient objectivity. And right now it's all deep background stuff. Nothing solid. Nothing solid at all. You're best when you have the enemy right in front of you. When we know who the guilty parties are, we'll bring you in for some fire and brimstone. Until then, you're better served dealing with something with an archaeological bent close to your current location. You seem to have had a lot of dealings with archaeology lately."

"I'm going to need backup."

"Already arranged. A French national by the name of Gaspard Morel from the Mexico City Interpol office. He speaks Spanish fluently, did a stint in the French Foreign Legion, and is familiar with Latin American politics and the criminal underworld. He doesn't have any experience in covert ops, however, which is why we need a CIA operative."

"That's because Interpol doesn't do covert ops. Why the change of heart?"

Wallace gave a bitter smile. "They're coming around to the realization that playing by the book doesn't always achieve results."

"I take it that the need for covert ops means we won't be informing the Peruvian government of our intentions?"

"The Peruvian government is a leaky boat, and a sinking one. We can't run the risk."

Jacob had a fleeting thought of that beach, and Gabriella. "All right. I'll do it."

"Good. The local field office in Lima will outfit you and can be called upon in an extreme emergency, but it's never been a large office, and right now with civil unrest brewing and a potential coup by the generals, we need every man monitoring the situation. We have to know when the coup is planned and if we need to evacuate our civilians. The embassy has already sent home any personnel not deemed vital to operations."

Jacob laughed. "You're always sending me to choice real estate. I'm not familiar with the Amazon, though."

"Gaspard Morel has spent time down there. He should be a good asset."

"All right. When do I meet him?"

"He's already staying at your hotel."

Jacob laughed again. "You knew I would say yes, didn't you?"

His boss smiled. "I know you well, Agent Snow."

* * *

An hour later, over a bottle of fine white wine in the Frenchman's room, Gaspard Morel and Jacob discussed the mission.

Morel was a lean, well-built man of about thirty-five whose body spoke of coiled strength and barely contained energy. His black hair, styled like a model's, and his brown eyes spoke of the southern regions of France, and perhaps a bit of Spanish heritage. His gaze was direct, his words clipped, with no hint of the all-too-common condescension of the French when speaking with the Americans.

Jacob pegged him as a pro.

Morel pointed to a detailed map of the region, indicating a spot in the vast jungle just to the east of the Peruvian Andes. "The team disappeared just about here, in the region where the forested foothills give way to the Amazonian lowlands not far from the Ucayali River, a tributary of the Amazon. We can get a charter flight to Pucallpa, this town here, and then take a boat to get us as close as possible. From there, we'll have to walk."

"Won't we stand out? The locals might figure out what we're up to, and that might get back to whoever attacked the archaeologists."

The Frenchman nodded, his face grim. "That is entirely possible, but time is of the essence. The only quick route is the one the team certainly took. If we move fast and cut along one of the back trails shown on this infrared satellite image here, perhaps we can evade detection."

"The attackers might be long gone by now."

"True. We might only be picking up bodies."

"When do we leave?"

"Tonight. There's a flight going to Lima. We'll pose as tourists."

"All right. The field office said they'd equip us both once we get to Lima. You know this region better than I do, what do you think happened to them?"

Morel shrugged. "Impossible to say. Probably narcos. The forest canopy makes for good cover for cocaine production facilities. The team might have stumbled upon one of those. Of course, there's also the Sendero Luminoso."

"They're active in that region?"

"They've been kicked out of all the more populous zones. There's only a small hard core remaining, hiding out in the most remote areas and living off of the villagers. I haven't heard any reports of them being active in this area but it's entirely possible."

Jacob grimaced. The Sendero Luminoso, the "Shining Path," were a band of Maoist guerrillas who had been trying to stage a Communist revolution in Peru since the 1980s. For a time they came close to winning, terrorizing the countryside, killing anyone who worked for the government or who did business with the government. They were crushed in the early 2000s, but never entirely defeated. Now a few small bands roved the countryside, extorting the locals with "revolutionary taxes" and occasionally even helping cocaine traffickers for a cut of the profits.

The Sendero Luminoso hated all people from the First World, especially Americans, and also had a nasty habit of executing LGBT people for representing "bourgeois decadence." If the team had fallen into Sendero Luminoso's hands, all Morel and Jacob were going to do down in the Amazon was dig six graves.

Morel sat back. "We need to go to the airport in two hours. I suggest a good meal before then. It might be our last." Jacob raised an eyebrow. Morel smiled. "I mean, our last for a while. After we get to Peru, it's going to be camp food for some time."

Jacob nodded. "All right, but before we go, I want to speak to a colleague of mine. She's an archaeologist and might have some insight into what these people were doing down there. Come with me. You'll want to hear what she has to say."

Jacob felt like a coward. He wanted another moment with Jana before she left and never spoke to him again, and the only way to do that was to use the excuse of work. He knew she was dedicated enough to her career and the community of archaeologists that she wouldn't say no to giving advice, no matter what she felt about him. Having Morel there would ease things, keep her from saying anything Jacob didn't want to hear. Maybe they could end on a happy note.

CHAPTER FOUR

Jana couldn't believe the nerve of this man. She had told him she wanted him out of her life, told him to stay away so she could live in peace, and here he was knocking on her door a few hours later, disturbing her much-needed sleep, to ask questions about a new mission.

And he had brought along a stranger so she couldn't chew him out! Coward.

"Come on in," she said, making sure her words carried some of the reluctance and fatigue she felt. "I can give you a few minutes."

She emphasized the word "few."

They entered. Jana sat on the bed. Jacob took the chair by the writing desk, while that Morel person from Interpol—assuming that was his real name and affiliation, she didn't trust anything Jacob said—stood by the door.

"So an archaeological team has gone missing in the Amazon," she said. "These things have happened before. That's a job for the local authorities and the embassy. Why is the CIA involved?"

"The team was just east of the Andes in a sensitive region," Morel said. "When they radioed a distress call, gunshots could be heard in the background."

Jana felt a tug of sympathy. Archaeology could be a dangerous job, taking researchers to unstable regions of the world. People sometimes got kidnapped or even killed. It was always a sad day when a colleague got hurt.

Morel went on. "As I'm sure you know, there's much social unrest in Peru at the moment, almost as bad as Venezuela. Plus narco traffickers and perhaps Maoist rebels are in that region."

"So they called in the CIA," Jana said and sighed. "How can I help?"

Jacob spoke up. "We were hoping you could give us some insight as to what they might have been looking for down there."

Jana shrugged. "I'm a Roman specialist. That's way out of my region of study. But if it's the Amazonian region of Peru, I can think of two possibilities. First are Inca sites. The Inca were a vast civilization

27

running along much of the Andes before the arrival of the Spanish in the sixteenth century. They built extensive cities and trade routes, and while they didn't settle in the Amazon, they traded with the people there. Given the location you mentioned, perhaps it was a trading center in the Andean foothills to exchange goods with the jungle tribes. I don't think any have ever been found, so it would certainly be a big discovery. Yes, that might be it."

"And the other possibility?" Jacob asked.

"New satellite imaging technology has revealed previously unknown civilizations in the Amazon. Some built entire cities with mudbrick walls and earthen pyramids, plus hundreds of miles of roads and canals, all now covered by the jungle. One was found down in Brazil, another was found in Bolivia, just south of where the team disappeared. It's called the Casarabe civilization and flourished from around 500 AD to 1400 AD, overlapping in time with the Inca. Their largest cities are estimated to have had tens of thousands of inhabitants. Perhaps the team was looking for a northern extension of the Casarabe civilization, or maybe even an entirely new civilization. This field of study is all very new, just in the past few years. Before that, we had no idea such civilizations existed."

Despite her exhaustion and the presence of this annoying man who had taken her father away from her, Jana could feel her enthusiasm coming back. With all the new imaging technologies, it was a great time to be an archaeologist.

"Interesting," Morel said. "Did these civilizations have any gold?"

"Gold? The Incas had heaps of it. The Amazonian civilizations didn't, but would have traded jungle products such as feathers and fruits to the Inca in exchange for it. Many pre-Columbian cultures revered gold because it never rusted or changed color. They thought it was a product of the gods, and holy."

"So simple robbery might have been the motive," Morel said.

"It could be."

"Robbery perhaps by a Maoist rebel group labeled a terrorist organization," Jacob said. "This is why the CIA got brought in."

Morel turned to him. "We better hope it isn't the Sendero Luminoso. They're masters of guerrilla warfare and know the region well. Plus they're well-armed and brutal."

Jacob grinned at him. "We're well-armed and brutal as well."

The Frenchman smiled and nodded.

28

Jana rolled her eyes. Macho men. She'd had way too much of that in her life recently.

She stood. "Well, I hope this helped. Now I need to get some more rest. I've had a hard day." She didn't know what Morel knew about the last mission, so she didn't elaborate. "By the way, who was leading that expedition?"

"A Cambridge professor named Carstairs Nasby," Jacob replied.

Jana sat back down on the bed, stunned.

"Do you know him?" Jacob asked.

"Yes," she said, the word coming out quiet.

Carstairs Nasby had been teaching at Cambridge when she had spent a year abroad there in graduate school. She was working on her dissertation on Roman settlement patterns in the late Imperial period with the university's team of Roman experts. On a whim one day, she attended a lecture on Incan archaeology by one of the world's leading researchers on the subject—Dr. Carstairs Nasby.

While the Incas were far from her core research interest, all aspects of the past fascinated her and the opportunity to attend a lecture from one of the movers and shakers in the field was too good to miss.

Jana found his lecture gripping, and when she went up to talk to him afterwards, she found herself in a friendly circle of graduate students who specialized in pre-Columbian archaeology. The conversation moved to the pub, as conversations so often do at Cambridge, and Professor Nasby came along.

Nasby turned out to be an intellectual of the old school. The conversation soon moved on from the Inca to archaeology in general, and then further afield to the Stoic philosophy of Marcus Aurelius, the neo-Gothic architecture of Cambridge's colleges, and the subtleties of Peruvian cooking.

Jana learned that Nasby and this circle of graduate students met regularly at the pub or, when the weather was fine, strolled the pathway along the River Cam to Grantchester, a little village with a popular tea room.

She soon became one of the crowd. While most worked in a field outside her research interest, she found many of the Roman specialists couldn't or wouldn't talk about anything that wasn't Roman. Jana had never liked how academia pigeonholed people into narrow specialties and neither did Nasby and his crowd of budding scholars.

For her year at Cambridge, Nasby had been host and mentor, a scholar who taught her as much as or more than the professor she had actually come to England to work under.

And now he was missing in the Amazon, and Jacob had been assigned to find him.

"Damn you," Jana whispered. "Damn you, Jacob."

Morel raised a curious eyebrow. Jacob made his usual dismissive, innocent schoolboy shrug he thought was so disarming but was actually irritating to the extreme.

"What?" he asked.

"I know him. He's someone I care about. And that means I have to go with you. God damn it, Jacob. How the hell do you always rope me in?"

His face fell. "Sorry, I didn't know. I just came down here to get some advice on the archaeology angle. I didn't realize—"

"You didn't realize you were going to disrupt my life yet again?" Jana snapped as Morel looked at anything other than her or Jacob. "You didn't realize that yet again an innocent bystander is being affected by your macho bullshit?"

Jacob went pale, and immediately Jana felt sorry.

"I didn't mean it like that," she said in a calmer tone. "You're fighting the good fight. I know that. What happened in Greece wasn't your fault. But you keep pulling me into these missions. I haven't had any rest since you came into my life."

Jacob looked at the floor.

"Well, you don't have to come," he mumbled. "We weren't asking you."

"Don't you see I have to come? Nasby is someone I care about. I have to help find him, or if he's dead, bring his body back for a proper burial."

She remembered Nasby's wife, a petite Chinese woman who taught Mandarin and Chinese literature at Cambridge. Jana and the other graduate students had been invited over for dinner on several occasions. Mei Xing Nasby was as brilliant as her husband. The two were devoted to each other.

Morel shifted uncomfortably. "Um, are you CIA?"

Jana grimaced as if tasting something nasty. "No, I am not CIA. But the CIA has decided I should be."

Jacob raised a hand in protest. "The CIA never—"

"Oh, shut up, Jacob."

Jacob shut up. Morel looked even more uncomfortable. The three settled into silence for a moment. It was Jana who broke it.

"So what are the details of the mission? Can we count on any local help?"

Morel leaned forward and, looking more comfortable now that he was talking about work and not witnessing an argument between strangers, said, "There's a plane leaving for Lima in two hours. We already have seats. I can get you on it. If it's full, we bump somebody. Interpol gets to do that. I've spoken with the branch office there and they are getting us a guide, someone who knows the Amazon well. She's with Interpol and has worked with ... other agencies before. She comes highly recommended. You won't be the only woman on the team, which is good, no?"

"It will be a nice change," Jana grumbled.

Morel briefly glanced at Jacob and then back to her. "The guide will arrange all the details in country. The CIA field station in Lima will supply arms and Interpol will not ask any awkward questions. While the agency can be sticklers for bureaucracy, the office in Lima understands that rules need to be broken at times if we want to catch criminals. They won't ask questions about a civilian like you coming along. Now, please don't be insulted, Mademoiselle Peters, but I must ask this. Do you have any training? Can you handle yourself on a mission like this?"

It was Jacob who answered. "She's got training, and she can handle herself. Trust me."

The Frenchman nodded. "Good, because I have gone on missions in the Amazon before, and we will all need every ounce of our training to survive."

CHAPTER FIVE

Despite her trepidation about going on a new mission, her worries over Professor Nasby, and her irritation with Jacob, Jana slept through the entire six-hour flight down to Lima. All these worries fought with the deep fatigue she felt from the mission she had just finished, and fatigue won. Her father's training about a good soldier getting their sleep when they can had buried itself into her subconscious.

She awoke when the plane touched down in the early morning. She felt groggy, and wanted nothing more than to sleep another ten hours. Jacob looked the same. Morel looked fresh as a daisy. Apparently he hadn't spent the past two weeks getting shot at and beaten up by pirates.

They were let off the flight first and a local Peruvian Interpol agent escorted them to a charter plane, a little eight-seater Cessna flown by a CIA operative that had already been loaded with weapons and gear. Jana sat in the back, as far away from Jacob as possible, and soon fell asleep again.

She awoke a couple of hours later to find herself over the Andes. Peering through the window, she saw the Cessna was flying between two snow-capped peaks, the valley between nothing but bare rock except for some vegetation along the many mountain streams. She saw no sign of habitation.

Peru is four countries, and they couldn't be more different, Nasby had told the crowd once over pints at the pub. *The coastal desert is one of the driest in the world. Bury a body and it will mummify naturally. The sands will leach out every drop of the body's moisture in a matter of days. No need for special preparations like the Egyptians used. I've dug up hundreds of them. Beyond the desert lies the upper grasslands where most of the cultivation and herding take place, then the high Andes. Only the toughest can live there, because it's even less forgiving than the desert. Freezing, with fierce winds that can pick you up and toss you over the nearest cliff. And beyond that is another world. The Amazon rainforest, stretching from the eastern slopes of the Andes all the way through Brazil to the Atlantic Ocean. And what a change it is!*

32

If you ever have the good fortune to fly from west to east over the Andes, you will see a magical transformation.

And now she was about to see it, while flying to try and save the old professor's life.

Or bring back his body.

They passed through the valley, and the plane veered left to follow another valley before passing between two more peaks that hemmed them in like a pair of giant sentinels. The plane shook a little from turbulence, riding the great currents of air that swept between these massive mountains.

A couple of rows ahead, Morel and Jacob sat on opposite sides of the plane, both looking out their windows. The pilot, who had spoken little during the flight, hunched over his controls, deep in concentration.

Nasby hadn't mentioned if this sort of flight was hazardous or not, but judging from the pilot's posture, back hunched and knuckles white on the yoke, it wasn't a cakewalk for him.

And then the sight outside her window made Jana forget all about the pilot.

Because she saw it, the magical transformation Nasby had spoken about.

The plane passed over a high ridge connecting two towering mountaintops, and the arid land and bare stone immediately gave way to shrubs and grass on the other side. Jana craned her neck to look forward, and saw ahead of them the slope falling off to lower peaks and foothills, covered in thick vegetation, and beyond that a great green carpet of foliage that was the Amazon rainforest.

Her breath caught. It was every bit as beautiful as Nasby had said.

The plane continued east, and soon they left the mountains and foothills behind. Below them stretched only the forest canopy, unbroken save for the occasional muddy stream meandering its way through the vegetation.

"Stunning, isn't it?"

She turned and saw Morel leaning over her seat, looking over her shoulder and out the window.

"Yes, it is."

"First time making a flight like this?"

"Yes."

"I've made it many times, and I never cease being amazed by the sight. It is a pity your friend is missing it."

Jana almost corrected him about Jacob being her friend, then decided against it. For better or worse, they were a team.

"Why is he missing it?"

Morel grinned. "He's asleep."

Jana rolled her eyes. "Typical."

"You are tired too, yes? I think you were on a mission together quite recently."

"We can't talk about that."

"Of course not. But if it has anything to do with that terror group trying to release a bioweapon at Teotihuacán, then thank you. I've had malaria and yellow fever, and two bad diseases is enough for one lifetime."

Jana nodded and looked out the window again to admire the untouched vastness of the Amazon …

… and grimaced.

Just below them, a road had been hacked through the trees, exposing rust-colored topsoil. At the end of this road, a vast swath of forest had been cut away, at least a square mile.

"God, that's stupid," she muttered.

Morel dismissed this with a shrug. "They have to make money, no?"

"There are other ways to make money."

"Peru needs to develop. It is a shame that it has to be done this way, but that's life. In any case, we're not here to save the rainforest, we're here to save your friend and his colleagues. We will land in Pucallpa soon. I better go back to my seat."

The Interpol agent left. Jana continued to stare at the ruined stretch of forest until it faded out of sight behind them.

* * *

Jana stepped off the plane at the Pucallpa airport and straight into a steam room. It had to be a hundred degrees and the humidity a hundred percent. The low concrete buildings of the airport, the distant line of trees, and the swollen sun overhead all seemed suspended in a muggy haze.

A short woman with broad shoulders walked toward them. She wore a simple green top and pants that looked Army surplus, and canvas jungle boots. She had the straight black hair, dark eyes and skin, and flat features of someone with mostly indigenous blood.

34

She walked up to Jana first and extended a hand.

"I'm Illary Huapaya. Pleased to meet you," she said in English.

"We can speak in Spanish if you prefer," Jana replied in that language. "All of us speak it here."

Illary nodded. "Good. I'll be your guide up the river. I was born not far from here and have lived in the region most of my life."

"Are you Quechua?" Morel asked, coming up and shaking her hand.

"Yes."

"Then you are descended from the Inca," Morel said with a smile. "We might be seeing one of your ancestors' ancient sites on this trip."

"Here in the jungle? Not likely. Is that what the archaeologists were looking for?"

"To be honest," Jana said, "we aren't sure what they were looking for. That's unusual for Professor Nasby. I knew him, and he always talked enthusiastically about his projects."

Jacob came out of the plane, rubbing his eyes.

"Who's the sleepyhead?" Illary asked, smiling.

"Jacob Snow, CIA," he told her.

"And I'm Gaspard Morel with Interpol."

"I've read your file, Monsieur Morel. You have a lot of experience down here. That will come in handy. Have you two been in the jungle much?"

This was asked to the two Americans.

Jana shook her head. "I'm trained as an archaeologist, but sadly I've never been to your country before."

Despite all those invitations by Nasby. I should have come when I had the chance.

"I've been in jungles some," Jacob replied in that vague way he always did when he didn't want to reveal past operations. Given all the work he'd done fighting Islamist terror groups, Jana imagined he'd probably been through Malaysia and the Philippines, not that he'd ever tell her. She wondered if he had gone with her father during one of his many long absences from her life.

"Good," the Quechua woman said. "Let's get this plane unloaded and I'll drive you to the pier. I have a boat waiting."

"Does the crew know the mission?" Jana asked.

"I'm the crew. It'll just be the four of us. Let's get this plane unloaded. I've already convinced the guards to look the other way."

Jana paused, then nodded. This woman played a bit fast and loose with the law, but she supposed they needed to down here. What bothered her more was the fact that there would only be four of them against whatever lurked in the jungle. As Illary backed a Jeep up to the plane and they unloaded various crates, Jana wondered what that could be, and if two Interpol agents, a civilian archaeologist, and a CIA agent with an injured wrist would be up to the challenge.

CHAPTER SIX

The Ucayali River, so muddy that Jacob couldn't see more than a couple of inches below its placid surface, ran sluggishly toward its union with the Amazon. On either bank, the forest pressed in close, not leaving an inch of soil uncovered.

They had only been on the river for half an hour, and they had already left Pucallpa, a city of almost 400,000 people, completely behind. Now both riverbanks were an unbroken mass of greenery, and there were no other boats on the river. Most of the fishermen stuck close to the city, and most of the trade went downriver. They were going in the opposite direction, into wilderness. The heat and humidity pressed down on them, and from the jungle came strange cries of birds and other creatures Jacob couldn't identify. He'd been to the jungles of Burma and the Philippines, but he had never explored the Amazon.

Novelty was rare for him, having done so much, and so despite the lingering pain of his injuries and the hurt he felt at Jana's continued rejection, he looked around with eager, searching eyes.

He, Jana, and Morel sat in the back of a long fiberglass motorboat painted a dark forest green, hiding from the sun under an awning. The back was packed with gear and supplies, leaving little room to sit. A small cabin was at the prow, where Illary stood at the helm. This cabin could be converted into a sleeping space with two fold-down bunkbeds and mosquito nets hung over the doorway and windows, where they could rest away from the incessant insects.

Jacob slapped at a mosquito on his arm and studied the riverbanks. This whole river was a prime spot for an ambush. An entire regiment of hostiles could be hidden in those trees and he wouldn't spot them. While Illary kept close to the center, they were still within rifle range.

Or rocket-propelled grenade range. Last week, he'd been on a boat that nearly got sunk by an RPG.

That was only last week? It felt like a year ago. That was one of the advantages of the crazy life he had chosen. When you pack so much experience into so little time, it makes time go more slowly. It was, in an odd way, a method to extend your life.

Extend your life by constantly risking it? God, maybe Jana's right. Maybe I really am nuts.

But what would I do if I didn't do this? Work security at some shopping mall in Omaha? Some people just can't live a normal life, and you're one of those people.

And still, sometimes he felt a little jealous of those sleepwalkers whose biggest troubles were an irritable boss, a long commute, and arguing with their spouses over what to watch on Netflix.

Jana's voice took him out of his reverie.

"Being on this boat reminds me of Néstor and Eva. I wonder how they're doing up in Venezuela."

Néstor and Eva were an odd father-daughter team who made their living using their sailboat for less-than-legal but still morally justifiable purposes. Theirs was the boat that nearly got sunk by an RPG.

"They should be all right. That private dock they're at is protected. The owner pays off the local cops and the local criminals. Néstor told me he planned to fix up the *Searunner* and get the hell out to Belize or Florida until Venezuela sorts itself out."

"I hope so. I hate to think of Eva in danger."

Jacob cringed. The kid was only fourteen, although already an expert sailor and avid adventurer. Still, he would have never brought her into danger if he had known that a band of pirates would show up out of nowhere and try to sink their ship.

Another innocent bystander getting into trouble because of you.

"They'll be all right," he repeated, as much for himself as for Jana.

"You two sound like you've been on a lot of adventures together," Morel said, waving his hand in front of his face to ward off a curious dragonfly.

"All that's classified," Jacob said.

"Strange that an archaeologist would be needed by the CIA."

"The CIA does a lot of strange things," Jacob said.

Morel looked like he was about to ask another question when Illary stepped out of the cabin.

"We're on a long straightaway so I've put it on autopilot. Are you hungry? We didn't have time to stop for lunch back in town."

"The quicker we got through town, the fewer eyes to see us," Jacob said. "But yes, I'm hungry."

"So am I," Jana said. Morel grunted his agreement.

Illary squeezed to the end of the boat, stepping over crates that packed the space between the benches running along both sides. At the back, near the engine, was a large, shallow metal box. She flipped this open and started pulling out paper plates covered in aluminum foil. Jacob caught a whiff of spices.

"Bought all this at the best restaurant in town," the Quechua woman said. "I keep this box back here exposed to the sun to keep things warm. Watch it, the food is hot."

The three passengers eagerly unwrapped the plates and beheld freshly cooked fish atop beds of rice, along with plantains and colorful jungle fruits that Jacob couldn't name.

Morel let out a little cheer. "I was wrong, my friend. Dinner last night was not our last good meal. A pity we don't have a couple of bottles of chardonnay to go with the fish, but we cannot drink on the job. We are not Inspector Maigret."

"Is that a colleague of yours?" Illary asked.

Morel chuckled. "No, a famous detective of fiction by the Belgian writer Georges Simenon. Inspector Maigret ate well in all his novels, like we are now, and drank constantly. Despite this, he always got his man, and we will get our man, or men."

They dug in. The fish was tender and rich and, thanks to their guide's makeshift solar cooker, piping hot. Illary went forward to check the helm.

Morel was sitting next to Jacob, with Jana sitting opposite. The Frenchman leaned over, nudging Jacob, and said in a low voice,

"Our guide is pretty, no?"

"She seems capable too," Jacob said, "which is more important."

"Yes, that is the most important. Of course it is nice that she is pretty too. I wonder if she is amenable."

"Doesn't she count as a coworker?" Jacob asked, wondering if Jana could hear them. The rumble of the engine might mask the Frenchman's words, or they might not. Jana sat hunched over her food, eating as eagerly as the two men, but she could be listening.

Morel laughed. "Oh, that is too American. We don't act like such puritans in France."

Jacob nudged him back. "We're not in France. You don't want some Quechua family cutting your balls off."

"Hm, you may have a point there. They are very tribal that way." Morel lowered his voice still further. "What about your coworker? She is not my coworker. Is she amenable?"

"She's got a boyfriend."

Jana was seeing someone on her dig in Morocco. Well, she hadn't actually said so outright, but it was implied. The people trying to kidnap Jana had certainly thought they had a connection. They kidnapped the poor bastard in an attempt to get at her. Only some quick action by the Moroccan secret service had saved him.

Morel made a show of looking around. "I do not see this man."

"Don't try anything," Jacob grumbled.

Morel raised an eyebrow. "Ah! You are jealous."

"No, I'm not. Just don't try anything."

"Whatever you say, my friend. I will try my luck with our Peruvian lady friend while you stick to your own nationality."

Jacob's angry response got cut off when Illary returned to join them.

"This food is delicious," Jacob said, waving his hand over his plate to keep half a dozen different species of insect from landing on it. He had a feeling this was going to be a recurring problem.

"Glad you like it," she said, sitting down next to Jana. "As long as we're on a long straight section of the river here, I can finish my lunch before I have to go back to the cabin if I hurry. And I do suggest you hurry. I see you waving away bugs already. More will come, attracted by the smell, until you won't be able to wave them all away. At least we're out on the river and moving. If we were sitting at camp in the jungle, we'd be swarmed. So eat up."

That sounded like good advice, and they all ate in silence, waving away the bugs that congregated in increasing numbers. Jacob caught Morel casting the women a few glances.

Once done, they cleaned up and Illary went to the cabin.

Morel smiled. "I think I will go check out the instruments on this boat. One of us might have to pilot it if our Peruvian friend is busy with other things."

He followed Illary into the cabin.

Jacob lay on the bench and settled in for a nap. Jana sat on the opposite bench, looking over him at the far bank.

Jana looked troubled.

"Don't worry," he told her. "If he's still alive, we'll find him."

"Maybe."

"Tell me about him. It would be good to know about the kind of man we're looking for."

"He must be about sixty now. An intellectual and kindhearted, not arrogant or elitist at all." Jacob tensed as he saw movement right next

40

to her. A multicolored form slithered over the guardrail. Jana went on, not noticing. "He's one of the great scholars of Inca archaeology, with a deep knowledge of the entire region." It was a serpent, with black, yellow, and red bands along its length, and knowing the Amazon's reputation, probably poisonous. Not wanting to make any sudden move that would startle the creature, or startle Jana into any reaction that might make the snake attack, he eased his hand down to the 9mm automatic in the holster hanging from his belt.

Jana looked out across the river, not seeing the snake or what he was doing. "He's an avid explorer. Knows the jungle well and has climbed most of the Andean peaks. He can handle himself. But this time I think he might have bitten off more than he can chew."

The snake raised itself up, its tongue flicking in and out toward Jana, fixing her with its beady black eyes. If she made any sudden moves, it would strike. Jacob eased the gun out of its holster. If Jana kept still for just another second, he'd get it.

If it struck now, there was no way he could stop it in time.

CHAPTER SEVEN

Jana looked out over the water, thinking about the professor she should have spent more time with, wondering if they would find him alive or dead. Jacob shifted on the bench, but she didn't pay any attention to him. She felt something tickle the bare flesh of her forearm but ignored it. Just another of the countless insects in this inhospitable place.

A blur of motion from the cabin. Illary leapt over a heap of crates, wielding a machete and coming right at her. Before Jana could react, the blade flashed down with a meaty *thunk*. A snake's head tumbled to the deck at Jana's feet. The back portion of the snake, fully four feet long, lashed back and forth, its simple nervous system reacting to the pain, unaware that it was already dead.

Jana screamed and jumped to her feet so fast she almost toppled into the water.

"What the hell!"

"A *naca-naca*, an aquatic coral snake," Illary said. "Highly poisonous. If it had bitten you, you would have had fifteen minutes to live."

"I was about to get it," Jacob said, holding up his pistol.

Illary looked at him. "Perhaps."

"Magnifique!" Morel cried from the cabin doorway. "You are as good with a machete as you are with a boat."

"Thank you," Illary said, tossing the head overboard and picking up the body. "This will make a good dinner tonight."

"I've never had snake," Jacob said, holstering his gun. "Does it taste anything like alligator?"

"A bit. I brought along some seasoning that will make it nice and spicy."

Morel smiled. "She's a cook too."

"I'm a lot of things," their guide said. "But right now I need to be a ship's pilot. We're coming to some narrow bends where logs and other detritus get stuck to the bottom. I need to keep close to the center so we don't catch any on the hull."

"I will help you in the cabin, to keep an eye out for them," the Frenchman said.

"I'm all right, by the way," Jana said, her heart pounding like a bongo drum in her chest. "Thanks for asking."

"I could tell you were all right," Illary said.

"They couldn't."

Illary shrugged. "Men."

Jana laughed. "Well, thank you."

"Don't mention it."

She went back to take the helm, leaving Jana and Jacob alone.

Jana turned to the CIA operative. "Why didn't you tell me about that snake? Did you see the size of that thing?"

"I didn't want you to panic. It might have bitten you."

Jana frowned at him. "After all the crap I've been through because of you, and you think I'd panic? When did I ever panic on a mission?"

Jacob looked regretful. "Sorry for underestimating you. You absorbed your father's training well."

Jana turned away from him. "Don't mention my father."

* * *

They motored up the river for the rest of the day. While no more snakes slithered onto the boat, they saw a couple of huge black caimans sunning themselves on the riverbank, and were constantly waving away mosquitos and other insects, especially when Illary had to slow the boat at sharp bends in the river, where logs and other debris accumulated. The mosquito spray they had brought with them from Mexico City didn't seem to do anything.

The hazy sun dipped below the foliage and shadows began to gather on the river.

"We're going to have to put in somewhere soon," Illary called over her shoulder. "Or we can moor in the center of the river."

"Which is the safer option?" Jana asked.

The Quechua woman grinned. "Neither. If we dock, we have to worry about jaguars, poisonous snakes, and poisonous spiders. If we moor in the middle of the river, we're more visible to hostile humans, and might attract caiman or more water snakes like the one we're going to eat for dinner. So pick your poison."

"Your call. As for dinner, I'm going to have some canned beans," Jana said.

"Snake can be quite tasty," Morel said. "I'm looking forward to trying your cuisine, Mademoiselle Huapaya."

"I say we stay on land tonight," Jacob said, studying a map in the dying light. "We're still far enough away from where the archaeology team disappeared that we portably won't run into whoever attacked them. But if they're on a boat, they might see us if we stay on the river. We'll dock and hide the boat under a bunch of branches."

"All right," Illary said, steering the boat toward the portside riverbank.

Just as she did so, there was a rustling of bushes on the bank and a man appeared.

He was short, no more than five feet tall, and completely naked. He had the complexion and features of an indigenous Amazonian. Stuck in his matted hair were several colorful feathers, and in his hand he held a bow. An arrow was in his other hand.

He didn't nock the arrow or say anything, he simply stood there with an unreadable expression on his face. Illary veered the boat back to the center of the river and picked up speed.

"What tribe was that?" Jana asked.

"Hard to say. They move around a lot, looking for game and picking fruit. They must have a camp nearby."

"He was warning you off?"

"Yes."

Jana looked back at the riverbank, but the man had disappeared.

"We're not going to get shot with poison arrows, are we?" Morel asked, slumping down in his seat to make less of a target.

"No. If they wanted to shoot us, they wouldn't have given us a warning. We'll go a couple more kilometers and then stop."

Night was falling quickly, as it did at the equator, and Jana looked around nervously. She didn't relish the idea of making a campground in the dark rainforest. She opened up one of the footlockers in the back of the boat and checked the several guns Jacob had gotten from the CIA office in Lima. The first was a high-powered rifle with scope. Jana wondered how useful that would be in the jungle. More practical were two Heckler & Koch MP5 submachine guns. This was one of Jacob's favored weapons, a compact but powerful gun good for close-quarters fighting. There was also a twelve-gauge, sawed-off shotgun with a pump action, plus three 9mm pistols. In a separate bag was a supply of flares. Another bag had several smoke, flashbang, and fragmentation grenades, and yet another had a few claymore mines.

Jana shook her head. This was supposed to be a rescue mission, and Jacob had brought a whole arsenal along.

Knowing his penchant for getting into trouble, they'd need it.

Jana took out an MP5, checked the magazine, and placed it in her lap where it would be out of sight of anyone outside the boat.

Morel looked at her, surprise evident on his face. "You know how to use one of those?"

"Yes."

"But you're an archaeologist."

"I told you she was trained," Jacob said, taking the other MP5. "Here, take the shotgun and we'll each take one of the pistols. Does Illary have any weapons?"

"She has a pistol and a shotgun in the cabin," Morel said and smiled. "She's quite the woman."

This is hardly the place or time for an office romance. I'd bet a thousand dollars Illary would agree with me.

Illary took the boat around a lazy bend in the river and then slowed. Jana immediately saw why.

A boat was moored in the middle of the river a couple hundred yards ahead.

It was a large river boat, four times the size of their own, with an upper deck, a spacious cabin, and a lower deck where a series of portholes shone. Several men stood or sat on the upper deck, drinking from bottles. A couple more leaned against the guardrail, fishing.

"Keep your guns out of sight, but ready," Jacob said.

One of the figures waved. Jana could see him as little more than a shadow in the dimming light. Illary cut the engine. Inertia kept them going forward, but they rapidly slowed since they were going against the current. They were still more than two hundred yards away, a difficult shot in this light even with a rifle.

Their ship's radio crackled to life, making Jana flinch. The voice on it spoke in English.

"Hello over there! We didn't think we'd see anyone tonight. We haven't seen anyone since the morning. I'm Brian, from Amazon Fishing Tours. I take tourists up the river. What are you guys doing all the way up here?"

Illary glanced at the others.

"Say we're on a botanical expedition," Jana suggested.

Illary grabbed the mic. "We're on a botanical expedition, a team effort between the Universidad de Lima and some international researchers."

"That's great," came the answer. "Want to come over for dinner? We got heaps of fresh fish and cold beer. My guests would love to talk to some local researchers."

"Let me consult with my colleagues," Illary said, obviously stalling for time. She looked back at the others. "What do I tell them?"

"Let's make our excuses and get out of here," Jana said. "We don't want to deal with any strangers."

"We should check them out," Jacob said.

"How often do fishing expeditions come up this river?" Morel asked.

"I've never heard of that company, but adventure tourists do sometimes come up here," Illary replied.

"I don't want to pass them by and have a potential enemy at my back," Jacob said.

"I agree," said the Frenchman.

"If they're a potential enemy, then boarding their ship will be a really bad idea," Jana said.

"We need to give them an answer," their guide said.

"If we do decide to go on board, we need to answer quick so they're not suspicious," Morel said. "Especially if they turn out to be criminals."

"We could be walking into a trap!" Jana objected.

"How would they know we're law enforcement?" Morel said.

"We should go," Jacob said.

"But—" Jana started.

Jacob cut her off. "Sorry, but I make the call, and I say we go."

Jana glowered at him, an expression that was probably lost in the gathering gloom. He didn't react, anyway.

Illary got back on the radio. "We'd love to come over, thank you very much."

She turned the engine back on and started forward at a quarter speed. "Look sharp, and conceal those guns. Let me do the talking. I actually do know a bit about the local botany. Just follow my lead."

"This is a bad idea," Jana muttered as they came ever closer to the mysterious ship.

CHAPTER EIGHT

Jana kept her eyes on the shadowy figures on deck, her hand resting next to the box containing the guns. The others had stowed guns in various hiding places close to where they stood or sat, and Jacob had also hidden a couple of grenades.

She didn't see any weapons on the supposed fishing vessel, but that didn't mean there weren't any.

She also didn't see any logo like tourist vessels usually had. Perhaps it was on the stern, which she couldn't see.

Or perhaps not.

Why couldn't we be in the Arctic, so I'd be wearing a lot of clothes I could hide a gun in?

That had never been a question she asked herself before Jacob Snow had come into her life.

Illary pulled alongside and put a rope around a bollard on the ship's gunwale. A couple of the men stood there smiling at her, their bodies tense. Jana noted she didn't moor the boat to the bottom of the river. Smart move. Pulling up an anchor was always a slow task. Cutting a line to the other ship would only take one swipe of that machete.

And it looked like she was bringing that machete along, carried in a sheath strapped to her belt. As she returned to the cabin and came out again, she brought the snake too.

"I have a present for your guests," she said, holding it up. More people came to the gunwale. Jana counted eight of them, all fit young men. No old guys on a fishing expedition? That seemed suspicious. Were there more people hidden belowdecks? At least she didn't see any guns.

"What's that?" one asked as he set down a narrow wooden folding staircase so they could climb up onto the taller vessel.

"A *naca-naca*, an aquatic coral snake," she said, climbing aboard. "It got into our boat and I gave it a proper reception."

Jana was about to follow when the two men shouldered past to go first. She rolled her eyes. That sort of machismo wasn't going to make any difference. On the other hand, Jacob was a master of unarmed combat. Morel, having been in the French Foreign Legion, could probably take on two or three untrained guys simultaneously.

Assuming these strangers were untrained.

They got on deck. A ninth man, whom she hadn't seen, flicked on a light in the cabin. Its glow illuminated the deck. Nine tight smiles and nine pairs of searching eyes greeted them.

The man in the cabin came out, quickly shutting the door behind him.

"Got to keep out the insects," he said. "Look how they're already batting against the glass."

True enough. More likely, though, you want to keep us out, Jana thought. *Why the hell are we doing this?*

"I'm Brian Garfield," the man from the cabin said, "owner and chief operator of Amazon Fishing Tours."

"Pleased to meet you," Jacob said, shaking his hand. "I'm Tom Miller."

This was one of his regular aliases, and it ran smoothly off his tongue.

There were introductions and handshakes all around.

"Jana Miller," Jana said when it came to her turn. The choice of the same last name as Jacob surprised her. It had just come out. Well, it would keep any of these guys from getting ideas.

"You two married?" one of the guys asked.

She almost said they were brother and sister, bit that down, and said yes.

Brian Garfield, or whatever his name really was, gestured to a long table set up just behind the cabin. A metal frame above it normally held a tarpaulin which had now been pulled back so they could see the stars. A bug zapper hanging from one of the bars sizzled so frequently it sounded like strips of bacon in a frying pan.

"Please, sit," he said.

They all sat and Brian busied himself unloading beers from a large cooler. A couple of the guys studied the coral snake.

"So this is poisonous?" one asked.

"Very."

"You're not going to kill us when you cook this thing, are you?" one asked. The laughter on both sides sounded forced. Jana squirmed.

"Oh no. I severed its head well below the venom glands." She pulled out some small packets from her pocket. "These will go well with it."

"What's that, coke?" one asked. The guy next to him gave him a somewhat playful, somewhat firm slap upside the head.

"Spices," Illary replied.

Brian gave an uncomfortable laugh. "Well, let's get the grill going. We caught a ton of fish today, and it looks like we're getting a side serving of snake!"

He and one of the guests started unloading fish from an ice chest. Whatever else they might have been doing on the Amazon, they certainly had been fishing. They brought out enough to give this whole crowd second helpings.

Soon they got the grill fired up and fish and snake were cooking. Brian and Illary stood side by side, adding seasoning with one hand and using the other to wave palm fronds to keep the bugs away. Beer flowed freely, and everyone got in a jovial mood.

Or at least pretended to get in a jovial mood. Now that they had been here a while and nothing had happened, Jana began to doubt her suspicions. The strangers asked a few questions about their research, which Illary answered intelligently enough to fool a layperson like Jana, and hopefully them. Jana replied with general answers about academic life, something she was familiar with, and avoided any specifics about botany.

On their part, they all talked about their travels to other exotic fishing spots, their home life, and their amazement at being in the Amazon. It all sounded seamless, natural. Jana's doubts about their guilt grew.

Whenever you're in a suspicious environment and your suspicions begin to get allayed, her father told her once, *that's when you need to watch out. That's when the enemy will pounce.*

Brian put a plate of delicious-smelling fish in front of her, along with a second bottle of beer.

"Where's the bathroom?" she asked. "I need to wash my hands."

One of the guests, who said he was a lawyer in New York City, handed her a box of sanitary wipes. "We use these. Our water storage is a bit limited on this boat, and we don't want to filter the muck we've been fishing in."

Jana thought fast. "Oh, well"—she faked an embarrassed smile—"... I need to use the little girls' room."

The lawyer chuckled. "The deck below, at the stern. That's the back of the boat."

Jana almost snapped at him that she wasn't an idiot and knew what a stern was, but only said "OK." Better for him to think she was some clueless academic.

Assuming he did think that. She had no idea if these people were buying their botanist act.

"You need me to show you?" another man said, half standing.

Oh, crap.

"I'm sure my wife can find it," Jacob said in a tone that carried jealousy.

"Oh, right." The guy sat back down.

Jana moved off to the large cabin, closed the door behind her, and took the stairs down to the lower deck, casting a glance around the cabin as she did so.

Shortwave radio in addition to a marine radio. Machete. Flare gun. Nothing too suspicious, except it all took on a sinister meaning in this context.

The lower deck looked innocuous. Bunks. Fishing gear. Crates that supposedly held supplies. A couple crates of beer. A glass-fronted liquor cabinet showing an impressive stock. If this really was a tourism company, Brian took good care of his guests.

What she did not see were any weapons, and that made her suspicious. Judging from what little she knew of the Amazon, it would be foolish not to venture this far into it without at least a shotgun. Professor Nasby used to joke about that.

"British gun laws being what they are, I don't own a firearm in my own country, but my house in Lima is equipped with a small arsenal."

She found the bathroom, opened the door, and gave a nervous glance back at the stairs. Had she heard movement in the cabin? Hard to tell. The sound of conversation and laughter carried down to her from the upper deck. A careful man could follow her without being heard.

She tiptoed back to the bottom of the stairs, didn't see anyone, and tiptoed back to the stern.

Am I getting paranoid? I would have never suspected these guys a couple of months ago.

A couple of months ago, I didn't have Jacob Snow in my life. You got to be paranoid if you're going to hang out with that guy.

She had less than a minute before the supposed fishermen upstairs got suspicious. If she was going to snoop, she'd better make it snappy.

Jana moved to one of the bunks, where a row of sleeping bags took up the space below the bottom bed and the floor. She moved these aside and found a metal footlocker behind them.

She pulled it out. It was heavy and scraped on the floor, making Jana cringe. She hoped they didn't hear that up there. She opened it a crack and peeked in.

Rifles. At least six of them, and more guns beneath. Her blood went cold.

She didn't take the time to look further. She'd learned what she came here to learn.

Jana pushed the footlocker back underneath the bunk with another incriminatingly loud scrape, rearranged the sleeping bags the way she remembered them, and headed for the stairs.

Then she stopped.

Details.

She hurried back to the bathroom, flushed the toilet, and was immediately glad she did. Brian hadn't maintained it as well as the rest of the ship and it made a loud rushing and clanking that the entire ship must have heard.

She squared her shoulders and took a deep breath. Now she had to put on her best poker face and somehow warn the others.

Briefly Jana considered grabbing one of the guns and holding it up, demanding to know what they were doing so heavily armed on what was supposed to be a fishing trip. Then she discarded that idea. She felt sure they had a pistol or two concealed on the upper deck or on their person. She wanted to avoid a gunfight where her side would be outnumbered, and she didn't want to lose the element of surprise.

So she tried to relax as she walked up the stairs to the cabin. No one was inside. Good. She probably hadn't been spied on.

I'll find out when I rejoin the others. If I don't take a bullet right away, I'll be safe for the moment.

But I won't be safe for long. No, these guys are going to make their move sooner rather than later.

CHAPTER NINE

Jana smiled as she returned to the table, sitting down. Jacob had been sitting next to her, but was now gone, as were a couple of their so-called hosts.

"Where did my husband go?" Jana asked.

"I guess back to his boat to fetch something," one of them said, studying her with an even gaze.

She wanted to ask where the other two went, but couldn't think of an excuse. She started to eat, eyes roving around.

Then she spotted a shadow through the windows of the cabin, standing at the prow. It was so vague she couldn't tell if it was Jacob or someone else. Illary sat opposite her and one place to the right. Jana moved her foot below the table and stepped on Illary's foot, pressing hard.

Illary caught her eye. Jana pressed against her foot three times rapidly, then three times slowly, then three times rapidly.

Dot dot dot, dash dash dash, dot dot dot. Morse code for SOS. Yet another skill she had learned from her father.

But would Illary know what it meant? Maybe just the surreptitious contact would signal enough.

The Quechua guide made the briefest of eye contact, something most people at the table would have missed, and if any had seen, wouldn't be able to tell the meaning of.

But Jana did. Illary's look had said, *I got your message loud and clear.*

Gaspard Morel sat next to Illary, out of reach of Jana's foot. He was turned away, telling some fishing story to a couple of the men, who pretended an interest. Their expressions looked so real, so convincing. They may even really be avid fishermen.

But they were so much more.

Just as Morel got to the end of the story, telling how he finally pulled in a swordfish in the Atlantic after a hard fight, he turned and raised his drink to Illary, who raised her own in turn.

That was a signal. Illary did the same thing to Morel as I did to her.

Now I just got to figure out how we're going to get the hell out of here.

Jana made a show of finishing her beer, tipping it up and putting her head way back. Then she put it down on the table with a clank.

"Want another?" one of the guys asked.

Trying to get me drunk? I didn't fall for that in college, and I'm not going to fall for that now.

"I got something better," Jana replied. "We have some champagne in our boat. We were saving it for a special occasion, and"—she put her hand on the man's shoulder, and his eyes sparked with interest—"meeting you guys is definitely a special occasion."

"Oh, you're too kind," he said. "But we have some champagne here. No need for you to get your own."

But Jana was already standing up.

"No, seriously," he went on, "you cooked us the snake and told us all your stories, you—"

"And you cooked us fish and gave us beer. It's the least we can do. I'll just be a minute."

Jana moved to the gunwale. She thought she heard the start of another objection, but it cut off. She resisted the urge to look behind her as the table grew quiet, then burst out with false conversation again. Illary and Morel would have her back. She hoped.

If these people keep up the façade for just a minute, we can maybe get out of here. They're suspicious, but maybe they still half believe the botanist story. Maybe we can get out of here with our lives.

Jacob disappearing must have made them wonder, though.

She got onto the little foldable staircase and stepped down into the boat. She made a beeline for the guns hidden in the crate at the stern …

… and never made it.

A shadow moved inside the cabin. It froze, then jerked back.

Shit! That's not Jacob.

She clambered over the piled-up supplies, desperate to get to the weapons.

Too late. The figure had seen her, and her flinch of surprise had given away the fact that she had seen him.

He emerged from the cabin. She swung around to face him. The gun crate was just out of reach.

"Oh, hey," he said. In the dim light she could recognize one of the two men who had gone missing. "I thought I saw a snake go in here. Wanted to kill it. Save you from a nasty surprise."

"I've already had a nasty surprise." Jana balled her hands into fists, ready to leap on him if he made any wrong moves. She didn't see any weapons on him, but that didn't mean he was unarmed.

"Sorry to startle you," he said, edging further out of the cabin and closer to her.

"Back off."

"I think the snake is still in there."

"Back. Off."

The man jerked a little, then slowly moved back toward the stairs to his boat.

The conversation continued in the other boat. They hadn't heard them over there. That wasn't going to last.

"Move," Jana said, taking a step forward.

The man scurried to the stairs and up.

Jana stood there a moment, surprised. He had run too easily.

A sound behind her made her turn.

Illary stood there, her machete in her hand.

Guess I didn't scare him off after all.

"We need to get out of here," Jana said. "We—"

Her words got cut off by Morel leaping over the gunwale of the boat and landing on a crate with a crash.

"We need to move!" he shouted.

Shouts on the other boat. Two of the men appeared at the gunwale and looked down just as Illary rushed into the cabin to start the engine.

"Where's Jacob?" Jana asked, diving for the gun crate. Morel rolled over some other crates to get to the port side, where he reached under the bench. She remembered he had been sitting there before they met up with the other boat. He must have stored his gun there.

"Hold it right there!" shouted the stranger who called himself Brian Garfield.

There was the sound of rushing feet on board the other ship. None of them came down to Illary's boat, though.

Shadows flickered across the portholes of their lower deck.

"They're going for their guns!" Jana shouted.

She pulled out an MP5, all pretense gone, and aimed it at the two men still looking over the gunwale. Both ducked back out of sight.

"Illary, hurry up with the engine!" Morel shouted, pulling his shotgun from concealment.

"They cut the wires. I need a minute."

"We don't have a minute," Morel shouted.

More movement in their lower deck.

"Where's Jacob?" Illary called out from the cabin.

"I don't know," Jana said. "He'll show up."

"We can't leave him."

"He'll show up." *He always shows up, whether he's wanted or not. Right now, he's wanted.*

"I need another minute," Illary said.

Jana glanced over at Morel, who looked as uncertain as she felt. The strangers had been suspicious, and had cut the ignition wires, but they hadn't committed any violence.

Yet.

While Jana was under no illusions, and she had been in more firefights than she cared to count, she had never fired first.

"Jacob!" she shouted. No need for false names now.

No response. More movement belowdecks. Whispered conversation from the top deck.

Only a matter of moments now.

We need a bit more time.

Gritting her teeth, Jana flicked off the safety and fired a short burst through the nearest porthole. Then she shifted her aim, fired another burst through the one next to it, followed by a third burst through another porthole.

Shouts from the other boat. Jana felt sure she hadn't hit anyone. No one had been at the first porthole, and they had probably all hit the deck after her first bullet crashed through the glass.

For that, she felt grateful. She didn't want any more blood on her hands if she could help it.

There will be more, she realized with despair. *Being on a mission with Jacob Snow, there's always more.*

The engine roared to life.

"Is he on board yet?" Illary called from the cabin.

A hiss from the other boat. Someone lobbed a flare over the gunwale. It landed in their boat, a blinding red that seared her eyes. It hit a crate, then rolled onto the deck.

Another came, this one coming to rest on a wooden crate. Blinking from the light, Jana could see the wood of the crate begin to blacken.

Jana grabbed the end that wasn't burning and chucked it back in their boat. Even that brief contact singed her fingers. She heard Morel curse as he grabbed the other one and threw it into the water.

"We need to go!" Morel shouted.

"Not without Jacob."

The muzzle of a pistol appeared through one of the portholes, the man holding it above his head to keep out of sight. Jana and Morel hit the deck.

Firing blind, the man raked the deck with bullets. One panged off a metal fitting close to Jana's head. Another crashed through the cabin window.

Jana emptied her magazine into the side of the ship just below the porthole. All compunction had vanished. This was now life or death.

"Let's go!" Morel shouted.

Jana felt her heart clench as she realized the engine was no longer running.

"Jacob, where the hell are you?" Jana shouted as she fumbled in the crate for another magazine.

There was a splash at the stern. "Here I am!"

"About fucking time!" Morel shouted. "Illary! Get this boat moving!"

No response came from the cabin. Jana stared at the bullet hole in the glass. It was right next to where she would have stood.

Just then, more fire erupted from the enemy ship.

CHAPTER TEN

Jacob clambered over the crates, dripping wet.

Bullets whined just over his head from someone firing blind over the gunwale of the other boat.

Jana silenced him by firing a burst right through the side of the gunwale. Neither ship was bulletproof.

"Where the hell were you?" Morel shouted.

Jacob ignored him. He needed to get to that cabin.

More firing. Jacob ignored that too. They could take care of it. He had one mission and one mission only—to get the boat moving and to get them out of here.

Just as he got to the cabin door, the engine roared to life. He saw Illary crouched before the console, adjusting some wires.

"The wires slipped apart," she said. "I never had to hotwire my own boat before. They cut the connection."

Another shotgun blast.

Without standing up, Illary hit full speed ahead. The collapsible staircase tore from the other ship's gunwale to clatter on its own before splashing into the water.

They pulled away, and as they did so, the enemy rose up to fire. Morel and Jana returned fire, making them duck back down.

Illary took a hard turn, the boat pitched far to starboard, then evened out. She sped upriver, away from the enemy boat.

"Where were you?" Jana shouted.

The sound of a grinding engine behind them made Jacob smile.

"Doing that," he said. "Unless they brought along a whole bunch of spare parts, they won't be chasing us."

"Is everyone all right?" Illary called over her shoulder. She steered the boat to the center of the river, and hopefully away from any underwater logs.

A few more shots came from the enemy boat, but they were dwindling into the distance and the bullets went wide.

They went around a bend in the river and the enemy ship was lost behind them. Only then did Illary turn on the boat's lights.

"Merde!" Morel shouted. "That was too close. Jacob, what the hell were you thinking disappearing like that? I didn't see you go. No one saw you go. Suddenly you were just gone and when people asked what happened, we had no excuse! And you do it just after Jana goes down below. Already when their suspicions were up."

Jacob shrugged. "I knew Jana had gone down there to search for guns, and I bet she found them. Those guys were suspicious as hell."

"I did find guns," the archaeologist said, examining her burned finger under the light.

"So I knew the shit was going to hit the fan, and so I slipped away to disable their engine. Here, Jana, let me put some cream on that finger."

He headed for the cabin, where a first aid kit hung on a bracket on the wall.

Morel pushed in front of him and grabbed the kit.

"Let me do it. You'll probably screw that up too," Morel grumbled.

"Excuse me?"

Jacob tried to stare the Frenchman down, but he had already turned his back.

"Here, let me help you, my archaeologist friend," he said in a gentle tone, opening up the kit.

Jacob snorted and looked away.

"So who were those guys?" Illary asked.

"No idea," Jacob replied. "I doubt they're narcos. They all sounded American. Maybe poachers, but then they'd be on land and not the river."

"They could be associated with whoever attacked the archaeological party," Jana said as Morel daubed cream on her finger.

"We're less than a day from the trailhead. Why would they hang around the crime scene for so long? You'd think they'd have powered that boat down to Pucallpa. They could have hopped on a plane and been out of the country by now."

No one had an answer to that. They continued up the river for several miles before Jacob called a halt.

"You sure they can't fix that engine?" Morel asked.

"I chucked four different essential parts into the river. Unless a caiman swallows them and pukes them back on their deck, they aren't going anywhere."

"We should post a watch tonight just in case," the Frenchman said.

Jacob couldn't argue with that.

"Fine. I'll take first watch, then you second, Morel. Then Illary, then Jana."

"And why do you get to decide?" Morel asked.

Jacob frowned at him. "You got a better schedule?"

Morel gave a shrug. "No. I just don't know why you think you are in charge."

Illary came out of the cabin. "If you're going to compare size, go to the prow so we don't have to see."

Jana giggled. The guide went to the anchor, picked it up, and heaved it overboard.

"We should be fine here in the middle of the river. It's a wide spot. Whoever's on watch, keep an eye out for snakes and caiman as much as you do for our American friends back there."

"Will do," Jacob said.

As Illary pulled down the bunkbeds in the cabin and put up the insect screens, Jacob did a search of the boat to make sure nothing had been damaged. Other than a few bullet holes and some ruined canned peaches that had leaked all over the deck in a sticky mass that attracted a swarm of insects, everything seemed OK.

The other three got into bed and switched out the light, leaving Jacob alone at the stern, keeping a sharp eye out for hostiles both animal and human. He kept an MP5 on his lap and a couple of grenades close by.

Soon his companions stopped moving in bed and breathed slowly and regularly. Now he was truly alone. Jana was still mad at him. Morel had some ego thing going. Illary seemed professional and distant. So it was just him alone with nothing but these damn persistent bugs to keep him company.

Sentry duty was one of the worst things about this job. He could handle recon. Fighting was fine. But sitting staring out into the night, ears perked for any unusual sounds (and what counted as an unusual sound in the Amazon?) he had far too much time for his mind to wander.

And when his mind wandered, all the bad old memories came back.

Afghanistan. Going feral. Aaron Peters saving him.

Aaron Peters. Who had he given the code to? The intel sure turned out to be correct, so whoever it was, they didn't lead him into a trap. They had Jacob's best interests at heart.

And Jana's.

But who the hell could it be?

Jacob had no idea, and mulling this over in his mind for the three hours of his sentry duty and coming up with no answer didn't shield him from the solitude and sense of failure he felt.

Gabriella was still dead, and Jana still hated him. The second problem didn't look any more solvable than the first.

Waking up Morel to relieve him came as a profound relief. He got into his bunk as quietly as he could so as not to disturb the others, and slipped off into a soldier's sleep.

No matter what the stress, no matter what the heartache, anyone who had spent a good deal of time in the field could slip off into sleep within a couple of minutes.

It was necessary, because you never knew what terrors the next day might bring.

* * *

"This is the trailhead," Illary Huapaya said late the next morning, slowing the boat to crawl along a straight stretch of the river.

They hadn't seen any sign of the gunmen from the other boat, or any other people for that matter. The river had seemed abandoned except for an increasing number of caiman, visible only as dark shapes sending out ripples in the water before disappearing below the surface, or a pair of hungry eyes right above the waterline, studying their passage.

"You sure?" Morel asked. "I don't see any trailhead."

The Frenchman was right for once. Jacob couldn't see anything but the usual green wall of foliage.

"It's there," Illary said.

"Did you check the map and GPS?" Morel asked.

"Of course," the Quechua woman said, then more quietly, "not that I needed to."

Jacob smiled at the irritation in her voice. Morel's attempts to hit on her had obviously failed, and that gave Jacob a smug sense of satisfaction.

"I'm going to pull in," she went on. "See how those big trees make an overhang? It will be a good place to moor, and they'll help conceal the boat. A few branches draped over the deck will do the rest."

They had decided, after tangling with the Americans, that it would be best to take the most direct route to the archaeologists' camp. Time was of the essence. They'd just have to risk it.

"Careful not to bump into the archaeologists' boat," Morel said. "They hid it so well I can't see it."

"It's not there," Illary said.

"What?" Jacob peered through the greenery. His trained eyes should have been able to pick up the coloring of the deck, of the ripples it made in the water as it bobbed along in their wake, but he saw nothing.

"No, it's gone," Illary said.

Morel shook his head. "Perhaps this isn't—"

"It is," Jana said.

"How can you know?" Morel asked.

"Because Illary says so, and she has way more experience at this than you do." Perhaps feeling she had been too harsh, she added, "Or any of us."

Illary eased the boat to the shore, moving slowly as the other three stood at the prow, guns at the ready, eyes alert for sunken logs, hostile animal life, or people. Jacob half expected a gunshot or poison arrow to come from the greenery, but nothing happened.

As they pushed through the overhanging greenery, startling a colorful bird that flapped away with a loud squawk, Jacob saw their guide was right. There was a trailhead here. A narrow but recently cut trail led into the rainforest.

How the hell did she see that from the river?

Always listen to the locals, Aaron Peters had once told him. *Even if they don't have as much training as you, their knowledge is priceless.*

The prow scraped against the muddy bottom of the riverbank. Morel leapt off onto shore, grabbed the line Jana tossed him, and tied it to a tree.

"Look," he said, pointing to an abraded section of the bark, "this is where Jana's colleague tied his boat. Oh, and look. Here's where someone tied another boat."

Jacob cursed. He didn't need to be told who owned that second boat. The people who had attacked the field crew. But had it been the men they tangled with the previous night? That didn't make sense. Why still hang around fishing, with the murder site less than twelve hours away? And why invite four strangers aboard for drinks and dinner? Wouldn't it be better to avoid people entirely?

While Morel moved a bit inland to stand watch, the rest of them unloaded their gear. Jacob and Jana both carried MP5s, while Morel and Illary had shotguns. Everyone carried a 9mm pistol and a machete. Jacob also brought along the rifle, claymores, and grenades.

All that weaponry, along with their food, water, camping supplies, and other gear, weighed them down too much. Just unloading all that crap had made the sweat pour out of him. Lugging it for a day through the jungle was going to be torture.

Maybe I should have become a mall cop.

They cut some branches and bushes and Illary expertly placed them so that they covered the entire boat. No hostiles would be able to spot it from the river.

Except that the hostiles already know where the trailhead is.

There was nothing they could do about that. After a last look at the river that was the only thing connecting them to the outside world and civilization, they headed down the trail.

While the trail was narrow, little foliage got in their way and they didn't have to use their machetes much. Illary stopped a couple of times to examine branches and creepers that had been cut.

"Someone passed this way within the past week, perhaps a bit more recently," she said, "and before that this trail has been cleared several times. It looks like Professor Nasby's team went back and forth along this route, probably going back to the boat for supplies. They most likely went back to town for supplies at least once, considering how long they were out here. Then there was a pause in the cutting, perhaps because the crew got busy at the excavation site, and then another group came later, within the past few days."

They moved on, staying on high alert.

But as the miles wore on, as the hours wore on, and the stifling hothouse atmosphere pushed them down, they began to grow careless. Jacob struggled against fatigue, trying to maintain a sharp focus at every moment.

He did better than the others. His Army Ranger training, his CIA training, and years in the field made him better at it than even an experienced man like Morel, and even a seasoned local like Illary, but after a time his steps began to shuffle, he tripped over roots, and his attention began to flag.

And that's when the pair of unseen eyes saw their chance and death came leaping out of the jungle.

CHAPTER ELEVEN

Jacob spun around at a rustle of underbrush. There was a flash of brown and yellow mottled fur and snarling fangs going straight for Jana.

The archaeologist let out a cry and threw herself to one side.

The jaguar, for that's what it was, missed her by an inch. It landed almost soundlessly just off the path, spun, and leapt again.

This time for Illary.

The Quechua woman brought her machete down a moment too late, and ended up hitting the beast with the pommel instead of the blade.

Even so, that saved her life for the moment.

Because the powerful blow just above the eye drove the jaguar's head down and its fangs snapped at air.

It didn't stop one set of claws from raking down her side.

Illary screamed and fell. The jaguar landed near her.

Jacob rushed in and swung his machete. The jaguar was too quick and darted to one side, then circled around a tree and came at him again.

Morel fired a shotgun blast at it.

The tree took most of the pellets, but judging by the way the animal flinched, at least a couple sunk into flesh.

Unfortunately, that didn't kill the animal. It only pissed the thing off.

It raced for Morel. Jana darted into the underbrush. That got her in the way of Morel's second shot and he didn't get the chance to fire again before the jaguar leapt at him. Then he, too, ducked to the side behind a tree and ran into the underbrush. The jaguar circled the tree and went after them.

Jacob dropped his machete and drew his pistol. He didn't have time to unsling his MP5. Even so, he was firing with his off hand. His right wrist was still too injured to trust his aim.

Not that his left hand was much better at aiming.

He fired and missed. The jaguar, either startled by the sound or going after easier prey, continued after Morel and Jana.

Jacob dove into the underbrush in pursuit.

For a moment he saw nothing, vines tripping him up and leaves slapping him in the face.

Then he caught sight of two figures darting between the trees in full flight.

For a moment he didn't see the jaguar, but then he spotted it, a dark shape moving almost invisibly in the foliage.

He fired. The creature vanished.

"Jana! Morel!"

He paused and listened. He didn't hear anything. His two companions didn't dare call back, afraid to reveal their position, something he himself had foolishly just done.

Where the hell is that jaguar?

Then he had a terrible thought. What if it was circling back to get Illary? She counted as wounded prey, and she was all alone.

He began to retreat back to the path. Much as it pained him to leave Jana and even Morel, who for all his arrogance was still a team member, they were armed and together. Illary was the one who needed his protection the most.

Assuming he could get back there. He took the chance of holstering his pistol and unslinging his MP5, and for a heart-stopping moment was without a weapon at the ready.

The jaguar didn't spring. Then he hurried back to the trail, looking all around him.

He found Illary sitting up in the middle of the trail, clutching her wounded side as blood trickled through her fingers, face contorted in pain. In her other hand she gripped her pistol.

"Where are the others?" she hissed through clenched teeth.

"Disappeared into the bush. I think the jaguar is still after them. I came in case it circled back for you."

"Thanks, but what we need to do is —"

Her words got cut off by a distant rifle shot.

Jacob and Illary exchanged startled looks.

Neither Morel nor Jana had a rifle.

* * *

Jana and Morel stopped. The rifle shot did not repeat.

"I think he got it," Morel said.

They listened for a few seconds more.

"That didn't sound like it came from the right direction," Jana said, "plus it sounded too far away."

They looked around them, guns leveled. Jana had pulled out her MP5 and Morel had his shotgun. Still she didn't feel safe, and judging from the look on Morel's face, neither did he.

The jungle closed in on them like a green blanket, cutting visibility down to a few yards. A jaguar could close that distance in a heartbeat, the last heartbeat its prey would ever have.

The shot did not repeat.

"He got it," Morel said. He breathed in, raising his head to call out.

"Wait!" she whispered.

"The jaguar's dead."

"We don't know that, and we don't know that was Jacob firing."

"Of course it was. Who else would it be?"

"If it was Jacob, then why isn't he calling out to us?"

Morel considered that.

"Well, let's get back to the trail and be quiet about it," Morel said.

They set out—in opposite directions.

They both stopped after a couple of steps and stared at each other.

"It's this way," Morel said.

"Are you sure?"

Morel looked like he was about to say yes, then stopped himself.

At least your ego doesn't get in the way of your survival instinct.

"Let's listen for a while longer," Jana said.

They did so, while Jana looked for signs of her passage through the rainforest.

She couldn't find any. She had never been much good at tracking, despite her father's lessons in the woods around their home, and this jungle seemed to swallow everything. The ground, a network of creepers and moss, was as springy as a yoga mat. The bushes would bend at one's passage and spring right back to their original position. It was as if the two of them had teleported here, never having moved an inch in any direction.

She turned to Morel and saw the same blank, confused expression she felt sure her own face carried.

They were lost!

"Do we shout for them?" Morel asked, his own hushed voice indicating his doubt.

"What about that gunshot?"

"I think it was this way," Morel said, pointing to a different direction than the one he had been going previously.

"Are you sure?"

"No."

"Damn."

Morel's eyes widened. "Hey! When we were running from the jaguar, we jumped over a log, remember? It had a side branch sticking up that I almost caught myself on. It's that one over there."

"Could be," she said, doubtful.

She saw a similar log in another direction, but the one Morel indicated did look more familiar.

Like you're going to remember correctly when a jaguar is chasing you!

"Wait," she said, "if we keep thinking about it, we'll run around in mental circles. Let's go with our first impressions."

"But our first impression was to go in opposite directions."

"Right. But we couldn't have gone far. Maybe two hundred meters, half a kilometer at most. Let's just go in an expanding circle until we spot the trail."

"That sounds like a plan," Morel said, looking hopeful. The hopefulness guttered out. "Assuming we can figure out how to go in a proper circle and don't veer off in the wrong direction."

"We just got to keep one landmark in sight. Let's go over to your log with the upright branch. We'll circle around that, keeping it in view. If we don't spot the trail, we pick some landmark further out and circle that."

Morel thought for a moment, looking doubtful. "That works, I guess."

They set to work. Walking side by side, the pair made a slow circle, keeping an eye out for any break in the foliage that would signify the trial, and for any movement that might signify friend, foe, or predator.

They didn't see any of that. Cursing, they expanded the circle, centering on a tall tree with a strange, split trunk.

No sign of the trail or any people. They expanded the circle further.

After many minutes, Jana wasn't sure how many, they heard low voices. They stopped and listened. The words came so indistinctly they couldn't make out the language, let alone the words. Jana felt pretty sure it wasn't Jacob and Illary, though.

Morel put a finger to his lips. Together they crept toward the sound.

The voices faded away.

Jana and Morel looked at each other. Had they been heard?

Jana resisted the urge to call out. While it could very well be their companions, something told Jana not to reveal their position.

The conversation resumed, clearer this time. It sounded like two men, and the cadence sounded like Spanish.

As the two speakers relapsed into silence, Jana leaned close to Morel's ear and, in a voice so soft she could barely hear it herself, asked, "Were they speaking Spanish?"

While everyone on their team spoke the language, they had gotten into the habit of speaking English on the boat ride up. Illary was fluent in English, and since two members of the team were native English speakers, that had become the default language.

Which meant that in all likelihood, they weren't hearing Jacob and Illary, they were hearing someone else.

They crept forward, squatting as they advanced to make as small a profile as possible.

The foliage thinned up ahead. They seemed to be coming to a clearing. Jana could make out something through the leaves, something that didn't fit.

They advanced a little more, and the foliage thinned enough that she could at last make out what for a while her mind couldn't grasp.

A stone wall.

And not just any wall, but one fashioned in the Incan style.

The Incas had been masters of stonework. Not content with merely using giant blocks to create thick walls and imposing buildings, they had developed an architectural style in which irregularly shaped stones fit into their neighbors like interlocking pieces of a puzzle, leaving a pleasing pattern in which there were no straight lines. Instead, the meeting points of the stones, aligned so well that you couldn't stick a razor between them, bent and meandered. While some buildings did use blocks that had right angles, the Inca preferred this far more complex method. No one knew why.

All Jana knew was that she had discovered an Inca building in the Amazon basin, where one had never been found before.

Discovered? No. She hadn't discovered it. The Spanish conversation had started again, not clear enough for her to make out words, but clear enough that she felt for sure now that they were hearing a pair of strangers.

The pair spoke quietly. There was a snap of what sounded like a magazine being put into a firearm, and they fell silent again.

Jana and Morel crept forward a little more and lay on their fronts, peering out through the last of the foliage at a clearing about ten acres in size.

The soil there was rocky. They must be closer to the foothills than Jana realized. No trees could grow there, only grasses and low shrubs seared by the powerful sun.

About fifty yards ahead of them stood a ten-foot-high wall of Incan masonry. It ran for about forty feet before curving around out of sight. From this vantage point they couldn't see how far back it ran. Jana suspected it was a *kancha*, a roughly rectangular enclosure with several buildings inside around an interior courtyard. A trapezoidal doorway stood near one side. They were at too much of an angle to it to see inside.

The jaguar lay dead about ten yards beyond the tree line, a large circle of blood explaining the rifle shot.

Just then, four men came out of the doorway. They looked Peruvian and wore camouflage. Three carried AK-47s at the ready. The fourth carried a hunting rifle.

Before Jana and Morel could react, they rounded the corner and went out of sight.

CHAPTER TWELVE

Jacob and Illary listened carefully, but did not hear any further shots. After a minute, Jacob helped Illary to stand and led her off the path and into a thicket where they'd be out of sight. The Peruvian sat and pulled a first aid kit out of her pack, wincing with pain.

As Jacob pulled out some antiseptic and bandages, keeping an eye all around him, Illary pulled up her shredded shirt.

Five scratches had made furrows in her abdomen. They weren't too deep, but they were long and looked like they hurt like hell.

He wiped off the blood, put on liberal amounts of antiseptic (who knew what kind of germs were on a jaguar's claws?), and put a large patch of gauze and tape on it. Illary took it all without complaint.

"You good to move?" he whispered as she put the first aid kit away.

"Well, I sure don't want to stay here," she replied.

Jacob grinned. "That's the spirit. Let's find Jana and Morel and then check out that rifle shot."

"They ran off in that direction," she said, pointing.

"You think you can track them?"

"It won't be easy in this type of rainforest, but I'll try. Let's get back to the scene of the attack. I'll pick up their trail from there."

They headed back to the trail, peering each way for as far as they could see and not spotting anyone, then walked along it for a few yards back to where the jaguar had leapt out at them. It was easy to find thanks to the scuffled tracks, trampled underbrush, a shred of Illary's shirt, and numerous drops of her blood.

Illary gave out a little shudder and gripped her shotgun tighter.

She found a trail that Jacob couldn't see but trusted was there, and moved into the rainforest.

They kept silent, Illary with her eyes on the ground and Jacob with his eyes everywhere else. A wounded jaguar might still be out here somewhere, and that made the creature exceedingly dangerous. There was also that mysterious rifleman. Those factors combined with the fact that the team was split up in a confusing landscape where it was easy to get lost meant they were in some serious trouble.

It was so often like this. Peace and order suddenly shattered, and the mission went sideways with a pile of new problems.

And it almost always meant that someone's life was on the line.

What had Jana said, something about getting as far away from him as possible in order to save her own life?

And now she was out in the Amazon rainforest, possibly lost, possibly captured by some unknown gunman, possibly being stalked by an apex predator.

Possibly dead already.

No. She can't be. I won't allow it.

Illary paused, peering around her uncertainly.

Don't lose the trail. Please don't lose the trail.

She started moving again, veering to the left. Jacob followed.

The jungle was a cacophony of sounds—the flap of wings, the cry of birds, the rustle of the canopy from the wind and creatures who lived aloft. Jacob strained to hear anything beyond this background noise, anything that didn't fit.

He soon heard it.

The clink of metal. Very soft and only once.

Enough to get his attention.

Jacob froze. Illary froze too.

A low thump, like a boot hitting a root, a sound they had made themselves countless times when they didn't take care where they put their feet.

The sounds came from their left and a bit ahead.

Without a word, Jacob moved that way, silent as the predator that nearly killed his companion. Illary followed, moving as silently as he did.

It wasn't long before they saw a break in foliage. Not much of one, but they were definitely coming upon a change in the landscape.

Moving behind a large tree trunk, Jacob peered through the gaps in the leaves and saw a trail.

For a moment he thought they had gotten turned around, before he realized this trail was narrower than the one they had been on. Well-maintained, though. Somebody was using it regularly. He looked up and saw that whoever cut this trail left it narrow enough that it didn't create a break in the canopy. That was probably deliberate.

He peered down the trail again. Figures emerged into view, four Latino men in camo and carrying guns. As they drew closer, he overheard their Spanish. Each man spoke with a Peruvian accent.

70

"It could have been Carlos," one whispered.

"It didn't sound like an AK," another replied.

"Who the hell else would it be? The archaeologists have been taken care of."

"That's what we got to find out. The cocaine isn't due for another day. Since when has Carlos ever been early?"

The four men came slowly along the path, which Jacob assumed intersected with their own at some point up ahead. They looked around, scanning the surrounding jungle like professionals. Jacob ducked behind the trunk before he got spotted. Illary crouched behind him, eyes wide.

Narcos. We won't be safe with these guys on the path.

Jacob took a deep breath and leaned partway out from behind the large tree.

The first burst of his MP5 took the front man full in the chest. As he staggered back, arms cartwheeling, Jacob moved his aim to the next man, firing a shorter burst this time.

It took him in the head. The narco jerked back, his knees buckling under him and he fell.

The third man had fast reflexes. He already had his AK-47 leveled and firing, his first shots chewing up the tree trunk, when Jacob's bullets stitched a line across his chest and he crumpled.

The fourth man fired a long burst on full auto as he fled into the underbrush, desperately seeking cover.

Too late. Jacob fired a final burst, cutting his legs out from underneath him.

Jacob rushed for the trail at an angle, keeping behind as much cover as possible in case there were more narcos coming up behind.

He didn't see any.

"What the hell do you think you're doing?" Illary shouted. "Those were narcos, you idiot!"

"Good reason to kill them," Jacob said, checking the three front men were dead while keeping an eye on the fourth, who lay groaning, his AK dropped out of reach.

He double-tapped one of the narcos who didn't look dead enough.

"Jesus! Stop!"

"It was them or us," Jacob grumbled, moving over to the fourth man. The guy rolled onto his back, wincing as a wave of pain wracked his body from the movement.

"Idiot! Asshole! *¡Hijo de puta!* This is a drug trail. You'll bring the whole syndicate down on us!" Illary yelled.

"Relax. For a South American cop you sure are finicky."

He leveled his gun at the narco.

"Talk," Jacob ordered.

"Your woman is right," he said, panting. "More are coming. They probably heard the shots. They'll be coming and when they do, they'll skin you alive, then take your woman and—"

"Where does this trail lead?"

"To some old ruins, like the ones in the mountains."

"Did the archaeologists come here?"

"Yes, but that's not their camp. They worked more inland. Ah!" Another wave of pain washed over him, making him arch his back. One of Jacob's bullets had shattered his left kneecap, another two had lodged in his right thigh and calf.

"Where are they?"

"I don't know. Someone attacked them. We stayed away." His upper body shifted now like a snake, a natural reaction to the overwhelming pain.

"You expect me to believe that? What did you do to them? Are any still alive?"

"We didn't do nothing. We have a shipment route through here, from the mountains to the river. We supply the towns, the logging camps. We don't mess with anyone who doesn't mess with us."

"But you knew about the archaeologists. Why did they get killed? What were they after?"

The man grinned, his eyes lighting up with a feverish glint.

"El Dorado."

He pulled his hand out from under him, where Jacob hadn't noticed he'd moved it, to reveal a compact automatic. Before the narco could aim it, Jacob put a round through his forehead.

"Damn!" Illary said, jumping back.

"Why are you so jumpy? You never been in a gunfight before?"

"Only twice."

Jacob blinked, confused. Then he remembered that this wasn't a CIA operative or combat veteran, but a member of Interpol. A police officer. Much of her time would have been spent on investigative work. Many cops went through their entire careers without ever getting into a gunfight. She knew how to survive in the jungle, and she kept her head in a crisis, but she didn't live the life Jacob did.

Hardly anyone did that.

Suppressing the sense of isolation he had felt for so many years, he gestured for her to get back behind the tree where they had initially been hiding. They waited there for a minute, scanning the trail and forest. No one came.

"We should check down that trail," Illary whispered. "Those ruins were their base. Maybe we can find some intel on the narcos."

Jacob smiled. She might not be a seasoned warrior like he was, but she was game.

They set out, paralleling the trail and almost out of sight of it. The foliage would make them all but invisible from the trail, while anyone walking along it would be visible to them. That gave them a decided advantage.

As long as the narcos didn't try the same tactic on the same side of the trail. Jacob and Illary kept alert.

The trail ran straight for a few hundred yards before coming to a clearing of rocky soil where no trees grew. In the middle of this stood a walled enclosure of strange, oddly shaped rocks that fit into one another perfectly. Jacob was no archaeologist, but it reminded him of photos he had seen of Machu Pichu, the famous Incan site.

Jacob glanced at Illary. From the look on her face, she was stunned. He guessed finding ruins like this in the middle of the jungle came as a surprise. Once they'd cleared the area of narcos and found Jana and Morel, he'd have to show Jana this place. Enthusiasm for the past always put her in a better mood.

First things first. They had to make sure no more narcos were hanging around.

He didn't see anyone, and didn't see any way in.

"This is a *kancha*," Illary whispered. "An Incan enclosure. Usually there's only one entrance."

"Is there a walkway along the top of the wall, like in a European castle?"

"That would usually be made of wood. My ancestors only used those giant stones for the walls. So the walkway would have rotted away by now."

"They might have replaced it." *That's what I'd do. It would make a perfect fort.*

They made a slow circle around the clearing, keeping deep in the foliage just like they did when paralleling the trail. They saw and heard no one, but finally spotted a strange doorway in the wall with a smaller top than bottom. It seemed there were no straight lines in the whole weird structure. He could see nothing inside except a stretch of grass.

Damn, this is not a good tactical situation.

They retraced their steps a bit to get out of sight of the entrance, and Jacob turned to his companion.

"We're going to have to rush it," he whispered. "Move fast in a zigzag pattern and don't bunch up with me."

Illary cocked her head and raised an eyebrow. "Just because I don't cold-bloodedly kill wounded narcos doesn't mean I don't know how to handle myself in a gunfight."

Jacob grinned. "Oh, sorry, was I mansplaining?"

"Is that an American term? I don't know it. But I think I can guess its meaning. Yes, you're mansplaining."

"Could you womansplain what we'll find inside?"

"A few buildings around a central courtyard, each with only one entrance. In the highlands there are many of these places. There was one near my village where we used to play hide and seek."

"Great, we have to clear a place that's a good spot for hide and seek."

"The sooner we do it, the sooner we can work on finding the others."

Jacob nodded. They edged to the limits of the greenery, paused for a moment, looking and listening, and then burst out.

They zigzagged across a wide open stretch of land, making easy targets for anyone watching. Jacob ran for all he was worth, adrenaline pumping, eyes searching for hostiles.

No shots came. They got to the wall and pressed their backs against it. Illary had made it only a fraction of a second after he had. Jacob nodded in appreciation. She was a fast runner and did not hesitate to do something extremely dangerous when the situation called for it.

Now for the tricky part. Leading his companion, he edged along the wall to the doorway. He paused, listening. He was tempted to throw a grenade in there, but the explosion would be heard even further away than all those gunshots. Plus if the narcos were hiding further in among the interior buildings, all it would do would be to announce their arrival.

Better to go in quick and quiet. He checked his MP5, then swung around the doorway and darted to the left, looking all around him …

… then froze as the muzzle of a gun pressed down on the top of his head.

The *top* of his head? What the hell?

A low chuckle mocked him, and Jacob felt the muzzle press more firmly against his scalp.

CHAPTER THIRTEEN

Jana laughed. From her hiding place in a doorway of one of the interior buildings of the *kancha*, she saw Jacob dart inside the main doorway, only to get stopped by Morel, who had hidden himself in a niche set six feet up in the wall beside the doorway.

They had feared the narcos' return, and when they had heard the gunfight just a few minutes before, they had prepared to ambush them if they returned to their base.

Now it turned out that Jacob and Illary had won that gunfight.

Jacob hadn't outwitted them, though.

The Frenchman laughed.

"Do not worry, my friend. It is only me. I thought you were one of the narcos. I apologize for the state of your underwear."

That gave Jana the giggles.

Illary passed through the door, smiling. Jana came out of cover.

"We found some narcos on the trail," Jacob said, nursing his head, and probably his ego too. "We took care of them. One said there's more on the way."

"They're using this as a base," Jana said. "We scouted out the whole interior. They have a camp here. We found some guns and ten sleeping bags."

Jacob and Illary went pale.

"We only killed four," Jacob said.

"We need to leave," Illary said.

While Jana wanted more than anything to explore this unprecedented discovery—no Incan site had ever been found this far east of the Andes—she knew they needed to leave. She and Morel had resigned themselves to a last stand inside this enclosure, but now that they had reunited with the others, they could get back to their mission.

"Let's go," she said.

"In a minute," Jacob replied. "I need to search their gear, see if I can find any intel."

"We didn't have time before," Morel said, "and we don't have time now."

"Guard the door, I won't be long. Jana, show me where that stuff is."

Jana led him through the rectangular courtyard, faced by five large buildings with stone walls rising ten feet high. She pointed out a wood scaffolding half built along one of the exterior walls where the narcos were obviously constructing a watchtower. Then she led him inside the largest building. Bedrolls and heaps of gear lay strewn around.

"They're using another building for cooking but all their valuable stuff is here," Jana told him.

Jacob started rummaging through the packs. Since she now had a spare moment, Jana's archaeological curiosity returned. She was standing in the middle of an unprecedented discovery. No way was she going to let this opportunity slip through her fingers.

She pulled out her phone and started to film, making a slow panning shot of the building's interior before walking out into the courtyard and moving along, trying to take in everything.

Then a small yellow dot up on one wall caught her notice.

It was a steel pin with the head painted yellow. A surveying marker. She looked around and found another, and a third.

Her heart skipped a beat and a lump came to her throat.

Professor Nasby had been here. He had discovered the site and surveyed it, making a precise map.

He couldn't have done that if the narcos had already been camping here, so they must have come later. Had they noticed the surveying marks, too, and tracked the team up to the camp, where they attacked them? Or maybe the criminals captured some of the team as they passed back and forth along the main trail picking up supplies from the boat.

Perhaps they'd find their answers up at Nasby's last campsite.

But if Nasby and his crew fell afoul of a group of narcotics traffickers, they were probably all dead.

Jana shuddered and tried not to lose hope.

Jacob came out of the enclosure.

"Nothing. What's that?"

He pointed to one of the markers.

"Surveying spots. Professor Nasby's team was here."

Jacob nodded. "One narco I questioned said they had come here. They said the team was searching for El Dorado."

Jana blinked. "El Dorado? That's a myth. Did the narco say this or did he say Nasby said it?"

"He wasn't clear. He was bleeding out. And if we don't want to end up like him, we need to get out of here. We'll learn more when we get to the camp."

"All right."

They ran back to the entrance to the enclosure, where Morel and Illary still stood watch.

"Nothing," Illary said before they could ask. "We've been lucky. Let's go while our luck holds."

Without another word, they hurried back to the main trail, retrieved their packs, and moved on toward their destination.

As they huffed along the trail, trying to put some distance between them and the narco base, and hoping they wouldn't bump into their reinforcements coming down the path, Jana thought over what she had heard.

It seemed clear that this gang had come across the archaeological team. Had they wiped them out just because they had stumbled across their territory? But the team had been in the region for some months, so the narcos had moved in afterwards.

She caught up with Illary, who walked in front.

"There's something I don't understand. The narco gang arrived here after the archaeologists. Would they kill them? Wouldn't it be better just to move their drug route somewhere else and avoid the attention?"

The Quechua woman thought for a moment. "They must have had a reason to attack. It doesn't make sense that they'd just attack when they could have made another route to bring cocaine down from the highlands. Despite their reputation, narco traffickers don't kill for no reason. They're businessmen, and attacking an archaeological team would bring unwanted attention, like you say. So I'm thinking that they had to come along this route for some reason; that they couldn't switch routes."

Jana bit her lip. "Which means we'll be seeing a lot more of them."

Illary nodded grimly.

"The prisoner talked about El Dorado," Illary said.

"But that's a myth, a confusion of an old pre-Columbian ritual."

"True."

"Care to share with the rest of the class?" Jacob asked.

"El Dorado literally means 'the golden one,'" Jana said. "The term comes from a ritual of a tribe living around Lake Guatavita in what is now Colombia. When they crowned a new chieftain, they would cover his body in gold dust and paddle out into the lake, where he threw gold artifacts into the water as an offering to the gods. Gold was a sacred metal in pre-Columbian cultures because it doesn't decay. The Spanish were entranced by the idea of a golden man, and when they plundered the Incan and Aztec civilization and found so much gold, they developed an idea of an entire golden city hidden somewhere in the Americas. Adventurers set out to everywhere from the Amazon to Colorado looking for it. But they never found it, because it never existed. It was all just gold fever."

"Your professor friend would have known all this," Morel said, taking up the rear of their little column and glancing over his shoulder every few steps. "Why would he be chasing El Dorado?"

Illary answered. "While Jana's right about the conquistadores exaggerating an old ritual into dreams of golden cities, the narco might have been using that as a term for something close. My people carried down traditions of a huge cache of gold artifacts we hid from the Spanish. Not for their financial value, but their religious value."

Jana sucked breath between her teeth. "That would explain why the narcos went after Nasby and his crew. If they thought El Dorado was real, that would make them a lot more money than smuggling cocaine."

Morel looked behind them again. "You're right. I suggest we pick up the pace. Night will fall soon and I'd like to pitch camp as far away from their base as possible."

* * *

The six men in camouflage stared down at the bodies of their four companions. Ants and flies crawled and buzzed all over them. In the heavy late afternoon heat, they already gave off the stench of decay.

They had returned from a tribal village a day's march away, where they had been trading for fresh game and fruit, things they didn't have time to hunt and gather for themselves, and had discovered their base at the old Inca ruins abandoned and ransacked. From there they followed the familiar path out toward the main path running from the river inland to the foothills.

They hadn't had to go far before they found their companions. They had been dead for a few hours at most.

A seventh man, short and indigenous, naked but for a quiver of arrows and a belt that held a machete in a sheath, paced around the nearby jungle, bow in hand and eyes on the ground.

"A man and a woman," he said in Spanish that carried the accent of an Amazonian tribesman. "Two of the four I tracked from the *kancha*."

One of the narcos, whom everyone called El Teniente ("the Lieutenant") because he was in charge, cursed and gripped his Ultimax light machine gun, a weapon of deadly accuracy that had a hundred-round drum magazine. It was one of the favorite weapons of the Peruvian military. He had bought it from a corrupt officer who knew it was better to do business with the cartels than try to fight them.

"They will not get away with this," he said. "Only four? We can take four, no matter how good they are."

"But who are they?" one of his men asked.

The Lieutenant shook his head. "I don't know. It isn't another cartel, not such a small group and not with women along. And they fight too well to be some gringo archaeologists. Maybe it was the people who attacked the archaeologists. Whoever they are, they'll pay."

The tribesman came running down the path, his bare feet hardly making a sound on the damp earth. They hadn't even realized he had left. He moved so silently they all called him La Fantasma, "the Ghost." None could pronounce his actual name.

"The four went to the other path and headed for the hills," he said. "Three white people led by a Quechua woman."

The others didn't ask how he could know this. La Fantasma's tracking ability was so good it was like he could see back in time to witness the people who had made the tracks. They had come to rely on him, and rewarded him well with the liquor and tools his tribe coveted. That had made La Fantasma a prominent man in his tribe, second only to the chief.

"How long ago?" El Teniente asked.

"A quarter of a sun."

"So about three hours. Let's go."

La Fantasma jogged down the path and everyone fell in behind him. El Teniente smiled. That was another remarkable thing about their guide. He didn't track like a hunter from the city or even a country village, stopping to stare around him, looking for the slightest traces and studying everything. He could jog along at a reasonable speed, merely glancing at the ground, and yet learn more from those tracks than any village hunter or city sportsman.

With a bit of luck, they'd catch up to those four by sunset, and then they'd have their vengeance.

CHAPTER FOURTEEN

The sky, briefly spotted through gaps in the forest canopy, was turning from a searing blue to a deep ultramarine. They would have to make camp soon. Jacob felt grateful. After the fights and the forced march, he was ready to sleep for twelve hours. Illary and Jana looked in even worse shape.

Not Morel. He walked along as fresh as a daisy. Well, not exactly fresh. He sweated and funked just like the rest of them, but it looked like he could keep walking for another several hours.

That left Jacob feeling equal parts impressed and annoyed. He bet Morel wouldn't look so chipper if he'd been through the wringer Jacob had been in for his last mission. If Jacob had been dealing with routine police work instead of getting his ass kicked by pirates, he could have marched for several more hours too.

But they didn't have several hours, not the way night came so quickly in the tropics.

"We should make camp," he said.

Illary nodded from her position at the front of the column. She gripped her shotgun, safety off. Everyone carried their arms at the ready after what they'd been through.

"We'll move into the brush, far enough that a fire can't be seen from the trail," she instructed. "We'll gather enough wood to keep a fire burning all night. That will keep most predators at bay, but we won't light it until it gets dark. We can't risk the smoke being spotted while there's still daylight."

"All right," Jacob said. Interpol had been smart giving them this agent as their guide. She knew all the angles. She reminded him of a Hazari tribesman who acted as their guide in Afghanistan when Jacob was in the Rangers. The guy was too young to grow the full beard prescribed by Islamic teachings, but he could climb like a mountain goat and shoot like a veteran. His family had been slaughtered by the Taliban, which were mostly made up of Pathans, a rival ethnic group, and he had sworn vengeance.

The kid had been at the village that day when the Rangers had run amok and Jacob had snapped. He often wondered whatever happened to him.

He often wondered if, during his murderous rage, he had killed the teenager and simply didn't remember it.

Jacob shuddered, feeling suddenly cold despite the humid heat.

"You all right?" someone asked.

Jana.

"Uh, yeah. Why?"

"You trembled. You're not coming down with something, are you?"

The look of concern on her face touched him.

"Uh, no. Just fatigued. Never got a chance to recover from that ass kicking the pirates gave me."

"Pirates?" Illary asked.

"Long story."

The Quechua woman shrugged and led them into the bush. They did not use their machetes and tried to avoid stepping on any twigs or small plants on the ground. They wanted to make their trail as faint as possible.

After moving in about five hundred yards, they stopped at a slight rise and pitched camp. Jana used her machete to hack away the undergrowth while Illary scouted the perimeter and Jacob and Morel gathered firewood.

All the wood they could find was damp with humidity and the frequent rains. No wonder Illary didn't want to light the fire until after dark. It would send up a hell of a lot of smoke.

Night fell shortly after they finished setting up, and they lit the fire and settled in to cook their rations on a pan they balanced on a couple of stones in the middle of the fire. Night seemed to close in on them. They couldn't see any stars through the canopy, and the buzz of insects, the cries of birds, and a million other sounds, along with the humidity and the stifling heat that nightfall did not lessen, made them feel like they were being buried.

At least they got to eat and rest. They had put up their tents carefully, and once they slipped inside them they would be free of the flying, crawling hordes of insect life they had spent the entire day slapping away.

"We'll have to post sentries," Illary said heavily.

Morel grimaced. "You are right. I'll go first."

"No, I'll go first," Jana said. "I'm too keyed up from that discovery to fall asleep just yet."

"I'll go after you then," Morel said. "Then Jacob, then Illary."

Morel looked at Jacob as if to challenge him to object to his making the decision. Jacob merely shrugged. It was as good a plan as any, and if agreeing to it soothed the guy's inflated ego, that was just fine by him.

Soon they finished their meal, cleaned the pans well away from the camp so no scraps of food would attract ants, and settled in. Illary immediately went into her tent. Morel did the same. Jana took one of the submachine guns and stood, about to disappear into the underbrush for a long, lonely vigil.

Before she went, she turned to Jacob.

"You feeling all right?" she asked in a low voice.

"Yeah. Why?"

"It's just that every now and then you have these little trembling fits. I've been seeing it for a while now. Did you get injured in the last mission worse than you let on?"

"No," he said quickly. "I'm just tired."

Have I really been having a bunch of them? He hadn't noticed.

Jana studied him. "We went through hell on the last one, and you got knocked out and beaten up and nearly drowned. If you're wearing down, or caught something, it would be better if I knew."

Jacob smiled. Thrust into this life only a few months ago and already talking like a soldier. "No. It's just fatigue. Really."

Jana shrugged. "All right."

She turned and stepped away from the fire.

"They're flashbacks," he blurted before she could disappear into the shadows.

Jana stopped and turned back to him. Jacob looked down, hoping she couldn't see him blushing in the firelight.

"I … get them sometimes. Ever since Gabriella got killed I've been having them more."

Jana hesitated a moment, then stepped forward and put a hand on his shoulder.

"I'm sorry. Are you getting help for that?"

"Help?" He looked up at her, suddenly angry. What did she think he was, some sort of clinical case?

Jana, taken aback by his reaction, said, "I mean, there's nothing wrong with talking to someone."

Jacob cocked his head. "Talking to someone? Yeah, they made me talk to someone. A lot of someones. All attentive, all sympathetic, except they had no clue what it was like to be outside the wire. You know what one of them said? 'I know how you feel.' Some civvie shrink actually said he knew how I felt."

By unspoken agreement they had walked out of the light of the campfire and into the underbrush, moving in a slow circle around camp. Jacob didn't want the others to hear, and despite having fallen into a deeply personal conversation with someone he had a troubled relationship with, they still had to keep watch.

"That guy was an idiot," Jana said. "But that doesn't mean you can't find someone else."

"Who? Who understands the crap I have to deal with? I know eight, maybe ten people at my level, not counting bad guys who would kill me rather than talk to me. But all those people are either constantly in the field or deep undercover or don't want to talk because they're dealing with their own crap and don't want to hear mine. Don't worry, though. I can keep it under control. It won't affect the mission."

They continued to circle camp, keeping the campfire in sight, a pattern of stars twinkling through gaps in the leaves. It was slow going. They had to test every step for vines and roots that could trip them.

"Mission, mission, mission. Jesus, I'm not concerned about if it's going to affect the mission. I'm concerned how it's going to affect you."

Jacob stopped. He couldn't believe his ears. "You are?"

"Just because I can't stand you doesn't mean I want you hurting."

"Oh."

He didn't know what to think of that answer. They continued their quiet creep through the jungle, slowly orbiting the camp like two planets in the cold outer reaches of a solar system.

They walked in silence for a time. Jana stopped.

"What?" Jacob whispered, looking around. He couldn't see a damn thing in this jungle even in the daytime. He was almost blind after dark. Why hadn't he asked for night vision goggles back in Lima?

"I just want you to know I don't dislike you for who you are, Jacob. Well, not too much. I dislike you for what they made you become."

You talking to me or your dad? he wanted to ask. Out loud he said, "The CIA saved me. And through the CIA I've saved a lot of people. I'm proud of that."

It's the only thing that makes the collateral damage bearable.

"Saved you or put you in a worse position? You could do anything, Jacob. You could be a great homicide detective or FBI agent, or even a bodyguard for some VIP. Why go around the world doing crazy stuff like this? You could have a real life and instead you go off to the ends of the Earth putting your life on the line."

Jacob couldn't help smiling. "You asking for me or for you?"

Pause. When the answer came, the words were soft, almost inaudible. "I guess I'm asking for both of us."

Jacob thought for a moment. He'd gone over this very same question so many times in his head, but he'd never had to vocalize an answer before.

"Part of it is because I can do some good in the world, and you and I have both traveled enough to know there's too much bad in it. Part of it is to atone for what I did in Afghanistan, and—"

"You stopped a massacre."

"By perpetrating another one. I was in the wrong just as much as they were. And … to be honest, those two reasons aren't enough. To be honest"—he looked at the gun in his hand, then around at the lethal jungle hemming them in—"I'm addicted. If I'm not doing this, I don't feel alive."

"Crap," Jana muttered.

"No, it's the truth."

Jana clicked her tongue. "No, I'm not saying you're talking crap, I'm saying 'crap, I feel that way too.' I thought archaeology was enough. Leading my own team. Writing articles. Traveling the world. Making discoveries. It wasn't."

Jacob chuckled. "What you were doing was the adventure equivalent of smoking weed. Now you're mainlining heroin."

Jana let out a bitter little laugh. "Except less healthy."

"At least we get to do some good."

"I suppose."

Jacob reached out, hesitated, then put a hand on her shoulder. "We do the good only we can do. Can you think of any of your colleagues who could have taken down a terrorist group in the Suez Canal, or tracked down pirates off the coast of Venezuela?"

To his relief, and a bit of excitement, Jana didn't pull away from his touch. She hung her head, though. "The only colleague I'm thinking of is the one those narcos might have killed."

"We'll bring him home, or bring him justice."

She looked up at him again. "Promise?"

The sudden vulnerability in her voice softened his heart.

"I promise. But I don't need to promise. Because if I wasn't here, you'd do it all by yourself."

He found himself leaning toward her. He couldn't see well in the dim light of the distant campfire, but he could see her tilt her head up, eyes closing, lips parting.

For a moment he wondered what he was doing, whether this was a good idea, but he didn't care. He moved closer …

… and the snap of a twig in the underbrush nearby made them both turn, crouch, and level their weapons.

A low rustle directly to their front. Jacob peered through the shadows and couldn't see a damn thing.

They crouched, as still as two statues, waiting, watching.

Another rustle, followed by a grunt and a snuffling sound.

Is that an animal? Jacob wondered.

He had taped a flashlight to his MP5 as night fell. Now he turned it on.

The circle of light fell directly on a wild pig. The thing squealed, turned, and rushed off through the underbrush.

Jana laughed in relief. "You should have shot it. We could have had bacon for breakfast."

Jacob laughed too as he turned off his flashlight. "Tempting. We don't want to give away our position, though. The narcos might be camped nearby."

"Yeah," Jana said, her voice going serious.

They paused. Jacob stared at her, but the brief light he had shone had made him almost night blind, and he couldn't make out her expression or even her posture.

Should I?

"Well," she said, "I better get back to patrolling."

I, first person singular.

"Yeah, well, I guess I better hit the sack. See you in the morning," he muttered.

Damn it!

"OK," she said stiffly.

"Try to shoot us a pig. I'm going to be dreaming about bacon now."

An awkward laugh from both sides. Jacob let out a breath and walked back to camp.

His thoughts and emotions tumbled around inside him as he got into his tent, zipped it up behind him, took off his boots, and got into his sleeping bag. It had been a long day, and an exhausting one, but despite his military training he did not fall asleep immediately. Instead he lay looking at the flickering display of light and shadow cast on the side of his tent by the campfire, wondering what had just happened.

Was it because he missed Gabriella? Was something else going on? Jana was an attractive woman, but her on-again, off-again friendship with him left him confused. They had come to rely on each other, and he had opened up to her more than any civilian, and yet she had this lingering hostility toward him because of her father.

And then, in the middle of the Amazon rainforest, he had started talking about things he never talked about with anyone, and she got it. She understood. Then the moment escalated and he made a move without even thinking it through.

Damn that wild pig. I really should have shot the little bastard.

Jacob wondered how Jana would act tomorrow. Impossible to tell with that woman. Too much going on inside her head. Her emotions bounced back and forth like a ping-pong ball.

Sleep, he told himself. *You need sleep. Tomorrow will probably be even rougher than today.*

The training kicked in. He forced himself to relax and clear his mind. Within a few minutes he drifted off.

But he didn't dream about bacon like he had joked, he dreamed about Aaron Peters.

Aaron was sitting against the mud wall of a peasant's house somewhere. His figure was vague, more of an impression than an actual image, and Jacob couldn't tell what he wore, and yet with that strange knowledge that comes with dreams he knew it was Aaron and that he couldn't leave the room.

A prisoner?

That vague impression of a head turned to him and spoke.

Jacob couldn't understand him. The words came out mumbled, distorted.

Jacob's own voice reverberated through his head. "What is it? Say that again."

Again Aaron Peters tried to speak, but his voice came out even more incomprehensible. Then the image faded and Jacob remembered no more.

CHAPTER FIFTEEN

The morning dawned overcast, casting the jungle into gloom. Jana crawled out of her tent, already bathed in sweat, to find Illary cooking breakfast. The two men were still in their tents. She could hear Jacob moving around inside.

Jacob, oh crap.

He had almost kissed her last night, and she had almost acquiesced.

Why the hell did I do that? she thought as she sat on a mossy log Morel had pulled to the campfire the night before to serve as a crude bench.

It was what he had said about being addicted to adventure. That had hit home. She had always been a bit of an outsider. Bookish and sporty at the same time, and fitting into neither clique at school. She had traveled the world and found it fascinating and somehow unsatisfying at the same time. Only when she really got out there, into the wild mountains of Yemen or the deserts of the Sudan and Chad, did she really feel like she was traveling.

Strange. All her friends and colleagues back home were amazed by how far she pushed her career and her life, and yet she never felt like she was pushing it enough. She felt like traveling the world as a leading archaeologist was somehow a cheap compromise, that it wasn't enough, that nothing could ever be enough.

Until that irritating man ripped her out of her old life and put her into a new one that gave her the only true satisfaction she had ever known.

What did one of Dad's friends say to her once?

"You're Aaron Peters's daughter, that's for sure. I see a lot of him in you."

That statement had annoyed her to no end. Now she saw the guy was right.

Illary came up, a tin mug of coffee in her hand. "Drink this. You look like you're still dreaming."

"Thanks. We should wake up Morel."

"He's already up. He's checking the perimeter."

"You've never worked with him before, have you?" Jana asked, lowering her voice.

"No."

"What do you think of him?"

Illary smiled and sat down next to her, taking a sip from her own coffee. "Too much machismo, but capable."

"That was my assessment too. What's his reputation in Interpol?"

"A good one. He only joined a few years ago. He's barely stopped being a … what do you call it in English? A rook?"

"Rookie."

"Right. But he's made some big drug busts and broke up a human trafficking gang in Guatemala. He knows what he's doing."

"So I guess we'll just have to tolerate him. I don't like how he looks at us."

Illary chuckled. "I've read about how things are in the United States. It's not like that down here. All the men look at you all the time, it doesn't matter if it's your boss or your coworker or your underling. The professional ones don't try anything more than that, though."

"Let's just hope Morel is one of the professional ones."

Illary nudged her. "If he isn't, we'll break both his hands, eh?"

They clinked their tin cups in a toast.

A low whistle came out of the underbrush, followed by a soft, "It's me."

Morel. Had he overheard?

The Frenchman came out. "I did several circles around the camp and checked the path. No one. That coffee smells good."

Illary pointed to a sealed plastic bag. "There are some cups in there."

Morel stared at her for half a second as if expecting her to get it, gave a little shrug, and went and got one.

"Seal it back up. The bugs will get in otherwise," Illary said.

"I've been in plenty of jungles."

Jacob came out of his tent, stretched, and yawned.

"Good morning, everyone."

He did not address Jana directly. He didn't even look at her.

"Good morning," everyone said, except Jana, who mumbled the greeting.

"We should get there by late in the afternoon," Illary said.

"Good," Jana said. "I'm tired of wondering what happened to Professor Nasby. I need to *know*. I vote for a forced march. We might need a lot of time at their campsite today."

Everyone nodded their approval.

Jana heard a patter above her, followed by the smell of rain. A few heavy drops made their way through the canopy to plop on her head and fall in the fire with a hiss.

Then the skies opened up.

It felt like she was in a shower. She and the others were soaked instantly. The fire died down to a smoky ruin.

"How long is this going to last?" Jana asked, having to raise her voice over the hammering downpour. None of them had run to the shelter of their tents. There was no point.

Illary shrugged. "Maybe half an hour, maybe all day. It's hard to tell. I can tell you one thing, though. We won't be making any forced march. The trail is going to be mud up to our ankles."

Jana shook her head, holding her hand over her coffee cup to preserve her drink. "All the more reason to get started right now."

They finished their soggy breakfast and broke camp.

The rain didn't let up for hours. They slogged through mud that clung to their boots and made every step an effort. The rain pounded down on them, forcing them to hunch their shoulders from the sheer physical force of it and obscured their vision down to a few dozen yards.

They kept on, walking in silence. They had to keep their guns wrapped in plastic. While modern firearms are water resistant, they didn't want to risk a jam or misfire. That made Jana feel vulnerable, but she reassured herself that any hostiles out here would have the same problem.

And she couldn't imagine anyone volunteering to walk anywhere in this rain if they didn't absolutely have to.

That got proven wrong several hours down the trail when Illary, walking in front as usual, raised a hand to signal a stop. She gestured for them to join her.

Jana got up to her side and through the rain spotted a series of footprints in the mud. The prints came from the other direction before turning down a narrower side path. That path ran thirty yards before circling a cluster of trees and going out of sight. The footprints were faint, just shallow oval pools nearly wiped out by the rain, but they were unmistakable.

Morel came up and studied them.

"Looks like a bunch of men wearing boots," he said in a voice so low the rainfall almost drowned out his words. "But how long ago did they pass? The rain is wiping out the prints pretty quick."

Jana looked back at their own prints. The heavy drops had already blurred the patterns of their soles and eroded the edges of the depressions they had made in the mud.

"I doubt these are more than fifteen minutes old," Illary said so low Jana almost didn't hear her.

"The path looks well-worn," Morel said.

"It's been used for a while," Illary agreed.

They moved off the trail and into a thicket, ears straining to hear any sound. Jana turned to ask Jacob what he thought they should do, and found him gone.

* * *

Jacob crept through the underbrush, paralleling the new path and stopping every few steps to look and listen. He had whispered to Morel to stay with the women and wait while he did a solo recon.

The rain, while no longer the heavy downpour that had ruined their breakfast, continued to make its incessant patter against the leaves and loud plops as it found gaps in the foliage to land in puddles on the forest floor. In the jungle heat, the water left a haze that was almost steam, lowering the already bad visibility. Water dripped off the brim of his hat, making the situation worse.

Jacob moved slowly, easing between the latticework of vines and creepers, jutting roots and trunks. With the rain and jungle sounds, he felt pretty sure he wouldn't be heard, but then again he would have trouble hearing anyone else.

He had seen how the path circled a cluster of trees. A good ambush spot. There might be a sentry behind them, although that sentry hadn't opened fire when they had passed into view on the main path. Perhaps this new group, whoever they were, had made it further away than Illary thought.

Or maybe they had heard Jacob and his companions, and lay in wait.

He kept moving forward, skirting the cluster of trees, crouching low and peering through the greenery.

There was no one behind them. The path, once it had gone around the trees, ran on straight as an arrow.

Jacob continued to circle the trees to make sure no one hid between the large trunks. They were of a species that had no branches lower down, so no one could have climbed up into the branches above.

Once he had secured his rear, he continued paralleling the path. As he advanced, he heard an irregular thumping coming from up ahead. He couldn't be sure, but it sounded like a sledgehammer on stone.

"Jacob."

The almost inaudible whisper made Jacob whirl around and level his submachine gun.

Gaspard Morel stood a few feet behind him, grinning.

Damn, for such a big guy he can sure move quietly.

The Frenchman came up to him and they leaned in close to have a whispered conversation as the strange thumping continued in the distance.

"I thought you were staying with the others."

"Illary found a good hiding place. Jana was worried about you."

The Frenchmen winked. Jacob resisted the urge to kick him in the nuts. He had enough enemies in this jungle already.

He jerked his head in the direction of the sound. Morel nodded, moved to put some distance between them so they could triangulate their fire, and they advanced at the same pace.

The pounding took on a different tempo. There were two distinct thuds, one a deeper tone than the other. Jacob became increasingly convinced it was the sound of hammering on stone.

It was still faint, though, and he hadn't heard it until he had gotten well off the path. He felt sure Illary and Jana couldn't hear it thanks to the muffling effect of the jungle and rain.

Like on the last side path, the ground rose slightly and the soil grew rockier. The greenery thinned and that made Jacob nervous. His eyes darted in all directions. The ground rose steeply to a ridge about ten feet higher than their current position. Beyond, it looked more or less clear of vegetation. The sound of hammering came clearly now.

Jacob and Morel got on their bellies and crawled forward. Mud smeared down their front and they had to flick away insects that crawled over them. Now that the forest canopy was breaking up, the rain hammered down harder on their backs.

They got to the top of the ridge and peered over. It fell off steeply, sloping down about twenty feet to a shallow valley on the other side.

In the center stood another Incan structure. It had stonework similar to the last one they'd seen, with large, irregular blocks fitted perfectly into their neighbors. Like the one the narcos had been using as a base, it had been stripped of the vines that would have surely covered it for the centuries it had stood abandoned.

Unlike the last place, it wasn't a cluster of buildings surrounded by a defensive wall, but a single building with a large doorway open to the jungle. Jacob had no idea what its purpose had once been and didn't have time to think about it.

He was more concerned with the group of men pounding away at one side of the structure with a sledgehammer and a smaller hammer.

Two worked the hammers, the bigger man with the sledgehammer splitting the stones while another man broke the chunks into smaller fragments. They worked on only one stone near the base. The wall around it had been torn down, leaving an open crevasse in the wall, the stones scattered on the nearby forest floor.

Another dozen or so men stood around. All looked South American. None were in camo, though. Except for two of them, all were dressed as workmen, with simple canvas pants, loose cotton shirts, sturdy work boots, and wide-brimmed straw hats. A few kept a lazy watch, toting banged-up AK-47s or old rifles. Even the two guys whaling away at the foundation stone had a pair of rifles propped up against a portion of wall they hadn't destroyed.

Two other men stood apart, and stood out. They were dressed in finer slacks and safari shirts. Each had a gold watch and they smoked cigarettes with an air of cool authority. They watched the two men with the hammers closely. Both had submachine guns slung across their backs, and pistols at their belts. One of them rested his hand on the butt of his gun.

Then Jacob spotted something else, something that got his attention more than the guns and the strange obsession with the foundation stone.

It was a backpack sitting at the feet of one of the men in charge.

It bore the logo of the federal government of Peru—a crest flanked by the national flag and bearing emblems of a deer, a tree, and a cornucopia. He'd seen that logo at the airport customs office and several government buildings in Lima and Pucallpa. There was some writing around it, probably for whatever bureau these guys were from or claimed to be from, but it was too far for Jacob to read.

What the hell was going on? Assuming these guys really were from the government, why were they with a bunch of peasant farmers destroying an Incan building that Jana said shouldn't even be here? She'd flipped when she had seen the last one down the trail, so wouldn't this one be equally rare and precious?

Morel tapped him on the shoulder and pointed down and to their right. A shallow ravine, cut by rainwater, angled down the far side of the ridge and close to the Inca building. Erosion must have filled the sides with soil, because it was thick with grass on both sides, and bare of plants at its stony bottom where a narrow creek ran, fed by the rain.

The perfect route to get close to those guys. As long as we keep to the center, we won't make any of the plants move. They won't know we're there.

Morel pointed to the pocket where Jacob carried his flashbang grenade.

Stun them, take them prisoner, and question them? You may be a jerk, but you know your job.

Jacob gave the Frenchman a thumbs-up and they wormed their way over the ridge, using a bush for cover, and down into the ravine.

They had to move slowly. The rocks had eroded down every which way and many shifted when they put their weight on them. Plus they were slick from the creek. Jacob and Morel found themselves testing every spot they put their hands or knees.

As they approached, crawling through a creek that could make them no wetter than the rain already had, the hammering stopped. Someone said something in Quechua, which Jacob recognized but couldn't speak, and someone else replied with what sounded like an order.

The hammering continued.

The creek was narrow enough they had to go one at a time. Jacob went ahead of Morel, and gauged that he had almost reached the point where the ravine cut closest to the mysterious building. He stopped, saw Morel several yards behind him, moving slowly and with care. Jacob edged into the grass on the side of the ravine.

Jacob pulled the flashbang grenade from his pocket and waited for Morel to reach his position. As the Frenchman crept along the stony bottom of the gully, Jacob slowly rose up and peered through the thick, high grass at the edge.

The two men had demolished the foundation stone and stood wiping their brows. One of the government men stood over it, hands on hips, with a pissed-off expression on his face.

What's going on?

94

A clatter of stone made him swing around. Morel had put his hand wrong, and a stone had slipped and smacked against another, making a splash at the same time. That made him stumble, making more noise.

The Peruvians reacted immediately. They swung around, leveling their guns. The two manager types backed off, barking orders in Quechua.

CHAPTER SIXTEEN

Jacob cursed and gripped his flashbang grenade, hesitating. If this really was a government group, initiating hostilities would be a really, really bad idea. He was down here on a search-and-rescue op, not to overthrow a foreign government.

But were these guys really with the Peruvian government? Even if they were, was smashing up ancient sites part of their job? Probably not.

A shout. One of the peasants pointed right at him.

Sharp eyes to see me through all this grass.

A gunshot. Jacob heard a bullet whine close to his ear.

That decided it. He pulled the pin and lobbed the flashbang. While the group had immediately spread out when they heard Morel, it would temporarily stun and blind some of them and hopefully make the rest dive for cover.

Jacob dove for cover too, throwing himself down onto the stones at the bottom of the gully and wincing as he landed on his bad wrist.

The grenade went off. Even in his sheltered position the flash of light was painful to his eyes and the shockwave felt like the first chord at a rock concert where he was standing in front of the speaker.

But it would give him a few seconds of grace. He sprang to his feet and, keeping low so his head wouldn't appear through the grass, pelted along the gully for the ridge.

Morel was almost over it, running for all he was worth.

Nice that you have my back, asshole.

By the time Jacob got to the bottom of the ridge, Morel was already up and over. To get to the top of the ridge and behind its cover, Jacob would have to reveal himself for a crucial couple of seconds.

"Cover me!" he shouted in English.

He ran up the slope, turning as he did so to let out a burst with his MP5, sweeping the weapon in a wide arc to encompass the clearing, where several of the men still stood or lay stunned on the ground, and the gully edge, where the advance guard had just arrived.

The recoil made his injured wrist sting. All his bullets went wide. Several men leveled their rifles or AK-47s at him and opened up.

But they were slow, and Jacob was just flinging himself over the ridgetop and out of sight when the first bullets came. A couple snipped off blades of grass near his feet, another thudded into a tree branch a little ahead of him, and then he got out of sight.

Morel was out of sight too. He'd vanished without a trace.

Jacob ran, boots slipping on the wet rainforest floor, eyes blinking from the daylong rainfall that decided that this would be the best moment to turn back from a drizzle into a downpour. He couldn't hear his pursuers, but he knew they were coming.

And they were Quechua. Locals like Illary. They would be able to track him and move much quicker than he could.

Plus he was outnumbered. Once the guys knocked down by the flashbang got up, he'd be *really* outnumbered.

Those guys wouldn't be down for long. Flashbangs worked best indoors or in narrow alleys and other close quarters, not in a field under an open sky.

He got behind a tree and glanced back toward his pursuers. Shadows flitted through the gray downpour, darting from cover to cover.

For a moment he thought they couldn't see him, but a three-round burst from an AK-47 chewing up the bark of the tree he stood behind disabused him of that hope.

He fired another long burst in an arc to cover the entire advancing line. He doubted he hit anything, but they did put their heads down.

And that gave Jacob a chance to run for it. He had to get back to Jana and Illary. They couldn't afford to be split up again.

He made it several yards before more bullets whined and thwacked through the rainforest. None came close. They couldn't see him. His pursuers were firing as they advanced, hoping for a lucky hit.

They'd close up soon enough, though.

He risked all by angling toward the side path, getting on it, and picking up as much speed as he could through the rain and mud.

Within a minute he got to the intersection with the main path running between the river and the archaeology camp.

No one in sight.

Damn. Now what?

"This way," Illary's voice whispered from beyond the green wall of foliage on the opposite side of the path.

Jacob plunged through the greenery and moved forward several yards, looking all around and still not seeing anyone.

"Psst," came a whisper, followed by a feminine giggle.

Both those sounds came from above him.

He looked up, searching through the leafy branches, eyes blinking as raindrops passing through the soggy canopy hit him full in the face.

A nearby tree, its trunk wrapped in vines, splayed out about ten feet up into several thick, spreading branches dense with greenery. A feminine hand poked out and waved. Another giggle.

That looked like Jana's hand. He wasn't sure that was her giggle, though. She wasn't really the giggling kind, although now that he thought about it, he had heard it a few times this trip.

More blind shots snapped out of the forest behind him. Jacob needed no further invitation. He got to the back side of the tree, grabbed onto a sturdy vine, and climbed hand over hand up into the foliage far above. He gritted his teeth as his injured wrist sang with pain, but he had learned to ignore pain. Getting caught would be far more painful.

He found the two ladies nestled into a bowl at the crux of several branches, surrounded by leaves and vines that hid their position perfectly. They looked quite comfortable and had even brought up everyone's packs. Jacob squeezed in between them, immediately aware of the warmth of their bodies through their drenched clothing.

"Nice spot you found us," he told Illary with a grin.

The Quechua woman put a finger to her lips.

Faintly they heard the sound of movement and whispers from the direction of the path. The sounds drew closer. Bracing himself, Jacob craned his head to find a little gap in the foliage to look down. He could only see a thin sliver of the ground below, but that was enough. He spotted one of the Quechua peasants gripping a rifle and stalking along through the rainforest as if he'd been born there. He looked from side to side, gestured at someone Jacob couldn't see, and passed out of sight.

The three of them sat in silence, trying to ignore the tickling on their skin from a dozen different species of bugs crawling on them, and shielding their eyes and noses from another dozen species of flying insect that buzzed all around them.

We've found ourselves an insect paradise. At least the little bastards aren't shooting at us.

A sharp sting on his cheek made Jacob grimace. He didn't dare slap at whatever that had been. He could hear hushed conversation almost directly below them.

98

Jacob dared another peek and saw a fleeting glimpse of one man passing back the way he came. Moving his head this way and that, Jacob found another gap in the foliage and saw a different man, also withdrawing.

Jacob looked at his two companions, pointed down, then made a walking motion with two of his fingers, moving his hand in the direction where the men had come from.

Jana nodded and held up five fingers. Wait five minutes?

He had a better idea. He mouthed the word *wait* and held up ten fingers.

Jana mouthed back something else. He didn't catch the meaning and so she repeated it.

"Morel." Followed by a questioning hand wave.

Jacob only shrugged. He didn't know and at the moment he didn't care. That idiot made a noise that brought a whole load of trouble down on them. Accidents happen. Fine. But he didn't have to turn and run just when Jacob needed some cover fire.

They settled back and waited. Jacob's cheek stung from whatever had bitten him, and he endured several more bites in silence. So did the ladies. All of them waved their hands around trying to deter the insects, but they were relentless and attacked them without mercy.

Jacob heard no more sounds of movement or talking. Still he waited the full ten minutes. Those guys might have set up a trap.

At last his watch told him the waiting period was over. He carefully looked through every gap in the foliage he could, saw no evidence that their pursuers were still around, and decided to risk a descent down the vine.

He swung out on it, felt a jolt of pain go up his arm, and looked around. He saw Morel standing by a tree nearby. The guy spotted him and gave a thumbs-up.

Nice of you to join the party, Jacob thought as he clambered hand over hand down the vine.

About halfway down, his injured wrist gave out on him. Suddenly he was falling. He tucked into a roll, impacted, felt a jab of pain as he rolled over the weapon strapped across his back, remembering the deep bruise he had received a few weeks ago from a similar move, and ended banging up against a tree trunk with a thud.

"You all right, my friend?" Morel whispered, coming up to him.

"You weren't so worried about that back at the archaeological site."

99

"Keep your voice down. I checked and they have withdrawn, but it is better to be careful."

"Why didn't you cover me?" Jacob whispered, picking himself up and rubbing his wrist. He needed to bandage it again.

"I only had a shotgun and a pistol. No good for long-range work."

"A few shots would have slowed them down."

"I am sorry, my friend. We both got away, no?"

Jacob shook his head and didn't reply. Instead he moved back toward the path, eyes and ears alert. Morel did too, moving off well to the side. Behind him, Jacob could hear the ladies coming down the vine, bringing the packs with them.

At least they're useful. Two out of three ain't bad.

Why the hell did Morel drop the ball? He's a pro. He shouldn't be making basic tactical mistakes like that.

At last the women joined them. Illary motioned for them to retreat deeper into the jungle, then parallel the main path before rejoining at some point ahead.

Jacob nodded his assent. While hacking their way through the uncleared jungle would be slow and exhausting, they couldn't risk bumping into the two groups that were on the prowl.

Two groups? Jacob thought so. Not only were they of a different ethnic makeup, the first group seemed more paramilitary in nature, and were involved in a drug shipment. The second group struck him as a group of locals led by a pair of city guys.

Great. Double the trouble.

Once they were on their way, moving between the thick growth and trying to make as little sound as possible, Jacob told Jana and Illary what they had seen.

Jana thought for a moment and said,

"It's incredible, a second Incan site in the rainforest. I bet Professor Nasby found both."

"Why were they smashing up one of the stones?" Jacob asked.

"An old legend," Illary answered. "Many people here think the Incan ruins hold treasure hidden during the time of the Spanish conquest. Some say that the biggest foundation stone of any building is hollow and contains the treasure."

"They couldn't have gotten that from interrogating Professor Nasby," Jana said. "He would have never believed something like that."

"He might have told them that to distract them," Jacob said.

"And destroy an ancient ruin? No he wouldn't."

"To preserve his life he might," Jacob suggested.

"You don't know Carstairs Nasby," Jana said.

Jacob shrugged and gave Jana an appreciative look. "No, I don't. I know you, though, and I know that while you wouldn't let an ancient site get destroyed to save your own life, you'd do it to save someone else's."

Jana bit her lip.

"You're right," she whispered. "We have to get to the camp as soon as we can, before those gold hunters realize the professor lied and go back to take it out on him."

CHAPTER SEVENTEEN

Jana and her companions arrived at Nasby's camp as the sky began to darken with evening. They were exhausted, covered in insect bites, and short on daylight, but Illary had steered them unerringly to the camp.

It didn't matter. As soon as they got there Jana realized they were too late.

The clearing was a large one, the underbrush cut back far enough to put the cluster of tents in the center out of range of any predators leaping from hiding and out of range of any tribesmen firing arrows. The professor had nearly been killed by an arrow on a previous expedition and Jana knew he harbored a lingering fear of dying from poison.

But his precautions had meant nothing.

Half a dozen tents lay collapsed in the center of the clearing, torn up and ruined. Off to one side were the remains of a bonfire. Atop a huge pyre of burnt logs and ash lay the seared flesh and burnt bones of several human beings.

Jana doubled over as if someone had punched her in the stomach. Gorge rose in her throat. Someone said something, but she didn't hear. Dimly she was aware of Morel and Jacob moving off to either side to scout the area. Illary sounded like she was doing something too.

Jana didn't look. She only had eyes for the horror that lay a few dozen yards in front of her. Swallowing the lump in her throat, she advanced on unsteady feet toward the funeral pyre. She shucked off her pack and gripped her shotgun hard.

As she approached, she saw more evidence of violence. The largest tent was punctured with bullet holes. A copper wire that would have served as a shortwave antenna had been torn down and lay tangled in the grass. She saw the transmitter half in, half out of the tent, smashed.

Something white and brown waved in the breeze on her path. She stopped and looked at it, and saw it was a page of archaeological notes, half burned, showing a sketch of an Incan pot.

She stared at it for a moment. The precision and detail with which it had been sketched reminded her of Nasby's hand. Perhaps he had done it.

Taking a deep breath, Jana walked the final few steps to the pyre …

… and stopped, frozen.

The bodies weren't so badly burned that she couldn't recognize a certain tall, lean form, and the swept-back hair of steel gray on the head.

The left temple had been shattered by a bullet.

Professor Carstairs Nasby, the leading scholar of the Incan civilization for the past quarter century, lay dead.

Jana choked back a sob and turned away, feeling sick. The mission had failed.

She stood for a moment, breathing heavily and staring at her feet, until she got herself together enough to turn back to the pyre. She forced herself to look at the bodies one by one, but they were either strangers to her or too badly burnt to recognize.

Jacob and the others had disappeared, no doubt searching through the jungle to make sure they weren't under threat. Jana had a hard time caring. A good man, a family man, a leading scholar, had been brutally murdered. It looked like five others had been killed too. She recognized at least one of them was a woman.

She didn't know their names. The list of researchers who had come to the Peruvian jungle with Nasby had been kept secret.

That was unusual for him. While he didn't seek publicity, Nasby was savvy enough to know when to use publicity to further his own ends. Archaeology relied on funding, after all, both from the government and from wealthy patrons. If he thought he had located Incan sites in the Amazonian jungle, he could have gotten all the funding he wanted.

So why the secrecy?

The words that dying narco trafficker had said to Jacob whispered through her mind.

El Dorado.

Ridiculous. Nasby wouldn't have fallen for something like that, but he would have worried that others might. Maybe he thought he had a chance to find those two remarkable sites Jana and the others had passed on their way inland, and feared others might think he had located the fabled city of gold.

He would have worried they would do just what they did do—kill them all in order to take the treasure for themselves.

But there was no El Dorado, no gold, only some remarkable sites that would change scholarly thinking of the Incan civilization.

Carstairs Nasby and his crew had died for nothing.

A movement at the tree line made her turn.

Jacob. He stood there, soaked and exhausted, his injured wrist bandaged, clutching his MP5. He looked at her with deep sympathy.

For some reason, that look broke the floodgates. She cried, and found herself turning away from him. She wanted to be alone with her grief.

Jana stood next to the burned bodies of her mentor and his field crew and cried for several minutes. When she finally wiped her eyes and looked around her, Jacob was gone.

She squared her shoulders, cleared her throat, and began to search the camp. While the rescue mission was a failure, they could still find those responsible and bring them to justice. Maybe she could find some clue that would help.

First she went to the largest tent, the one peppered with bullets. Like the others, the stakes had been pulled up and the tent had collapsed. She lifted the opening and looked inside. Other than the ruined radio she had already spotted, she saw an empty shell casing and some open wooden crates with packing straw scattered around.

Looking inside the crates, she found several fine examples of Incan pottery all jumbled up inside. They would have been neatly packed. Whoever had killed the crew had rummaged around in them, no doubt looking for gold.

So this had been the tent for storing artifacts. The notes should have been here too, but she didn't see them, only that half-burned scrap she had found earlier.

Jana returned to the pyre and forced herself to take another look. She didn't see any scraps of paper among the bodies. Had the notebook, or notebooks, been burned separately, or perhaps thrown onto the top of the pyre, for the pages to burn and flutter away in the wind?

She searched each of the other tents one by one. Besides bedrolls, personal items, some cooking gear, and other camping essentials, she found little. No weapons, no food, no first aid kit.

Whoever attacked the crew had taken everything they could use. So why burn the notebooks?

She paused, unsure what to do next. The rain continued to weep from the leaden sky. Something about this camp didn't seem right. This was obviously the main camp, judging from how much underbrush had been cut away. The trail from here to the river was well-maintained. The side trails to the two sites were narrower. Illary said they looked less used. Why not have the camp closer to the sites? And wouldn't the side trails to them be wider and better maintained?

They weren't the main object of the expedition, Jana realized. *Something closer to here was.*

But what?

Jana noticed that the camp was built on a slight slope. The ground wasn't as rocky as the sites of the two Incan ruins, but it wasn't the pure topsoil of the Amazon basin either. Her expert eye, accustomed to reading the ground, saw that there were many small stones that looked like they had eroded down from further up the slope. She recalled that the foothills to the Andes started very close to this spot. Not far to the west, then, would be rocky hills and ridges, getting bigger and more numerous the further west you went until you reached the tallest mountains in South America.

All of this was obscured by the rainforest hemming in the campsite. She knew it was there, though.

So the best place to look for Incan sites would be just west of camp. Those pieces of pottery had to have come from somewhere.

Looking that direction, she saw a path running off into the rainforest.

She started walking that way, so intent on finding clues to Nasby's discovery that she didn't think of her own safety, or even finding the rest of the team and telling them. The sight of Nasby's burnt corpse, left to rot and be rained on in an unknown patch of jungle, had caused her reason to flee.

She needed to find this site, see what Nasby died for.

Only one thing could distract her from her goal, and that was another piece of burnt notebook paper caught between the ground and a creeper close to the path.

She stooped and picked it up. It was only a quarter of a page, and entirely blank.

Swearing under her breath, she tossed it aside and moved to the entrance to the path.

Only then did common sense break through her determination. She shouldn't go off alone. Since there hadn't been any firing from any of the others, the chance that any hostiles were lurking around here was low, but she shouldn't risk it. Better to gather up the team and all go together.

She was about to go and do that when another piece of paper, caught amid some ferns a few yards along the path, caught her eye. Checking the jungle to the left and right and not seeing anyone, she crept forward to it.

This page was mostly intact, and was another drawing. It showed several pottery fragments, each painted with abstract designs or Incan deities. Jana didn't know enough about South American mythology to identify them. The colors were well-preserved despite the page being soggy. She carefully folded the page up and put it in her pocket.

Then another page further along the trail caught her eye, almost hidden between two roots. Checking the surrounding forest once again, she went over to it.

It was only a thin strip, barely the width and length of two fingers together. It was part of a journal entry written in Nasby's distinctive hand.

" … through the cleft at local sunrise the beams shine down on the entrance, invisible otherwise. How great, how brilliant the Incans were! To use the natural topography so cleverly, to find connections in the natural world to help them in the material one. They …"

Jana reread the fragment a couple of times. A beam of sunlight shining through an entrance? She knew the Incans were perceptive astronomers, using the heavens as a calendar telling them when to plant and harvest, and also as a sign of what the gods thought and intended for the future. Nasby had told her that at the famous site of Machu Picchu, the Intihuatana Stone, a natural stone outcropping near the highest point in the settlement, had been carved into a strange geometric shape of many faces and angles. It had taken years for investigators to puzzle out that these had been used as sight lines to important astronomical events such as the solstices and equinoxes, the rising of Venus, and the phases of the moon. It was a stone calendar and an astronomical clock, a brilliant scientific development of a complex society.

So this must be something similar, and judging from Nasby's ecstatic tone, something groundbreaking.

But what did he mean by "cleft" and "local sunrise"?

A sound behind her made her turn, thinking that Jacob or one of the others had come to join her, no doubt to chew her out for going off alone.

But it wasn't Jacob, and it wasn't one of the others.

A trio of South American men in camouflage stood staring at her from a few feet away. Each gripped a Kalashnikov. They looked like local Peruvians. One grinned at her, showing a gold tooth.

Jana, heart hammering in her chest, dropped her shotgun. Slowly, keeping her hands well away from the pistol at her belt, she raised her hands over her head.

The man with the gold tooth grinned even wider. All three raised their assault rifles to point at her.

CHAPTER EIGHTEEN

Jacob and Morel had been tracking the three men in camo for a few minutes now, creeping behind them through the rain as the strangers approached the camp. By a few looks and gestures, the two warriors had agreed to get the drop on them before they reached the clearing. Jacob wanted to take them prisoner and question them.

But just as they were about to pounce, Jana came wandering up the path. Now she had her hands above her head and faced the three men, who raised their guns.

Would they fire, or capture her? It didn't look like they had bothered to take prisoners with the archaeological crew.

Jacob and Morel needed to take these guys out.

But they couldn't fire. The strangers stood between themselves and Jana. A stray bullet could kill her.

They stood about twenty yards behind the three strangers, too far to take careful enough aim, and they didn't have time to close the distance before those guys made their move.

Jacob raised his MP5 and fired a single shot in the air.

It had the exact effect Jacob wanted. The three guys whirled around to face this new threat, and Jana dove to the side to get out of the way.

Jacob aimed at the man furthest from Jana, just in case.

His bullets stitched a bloody line up the man's chest, throwing him back to hit a tree trunk and sink to the ground. Morel took out the middle figure with a shotgun blast that also nicked the man next to him, who cringed from the pain, making his own shot from his Kalashnikov go wide. Jacob swiveled to take him out and was about to pull the trigger when another shot rang out. The man stumbled forward and fell flat on his face, a garish wound in the back of his head.

Jana lay on the ground, her 9mm in her hand.

Jacob's gaze roved over the three bodies. They were all dead.

"Damn, we should have saved one for questioning," he muttered.

"There was no time, my friend," Morel said.

"Hey," Jana whispered, pointing behind them, further up the slope.

Jacob and Morel got behind the nearest tree before they even looked. Jana did the same with another tree.

Crouching, Jacob dared a peek.

For a second he didn't see anything, then off to his far left, he spotted a shadow flit between two bushes. A moment later he saw movement to his right and front.

"Pincher movement," Morel whispered.

So he had seen the same thing.

Good for me you're not running away this time.

The crack of a rifle shot. A bullet chewed through the tree trunk just above Jacob's head, bit of wood thumping against the top of his hat.

Jacob ducked back.

"Did you see him?" he asked Morel, who had ducked behind the tree at the same time.

"No." He leaned back to give a quick glance to the left and right. "But the man to our right is already a bit to our rear, and I can't see the man to our left."

Jacob's mind raced for a plan. Just as he came up with one, gunfire erupted to their right. The tell-tale sound of an MP5 and the answering crack of an AK-47.

Illary had the other MP5, so she was in on the game.

Jacob reached around the tree, firing a burst blind, then popped his head around to fire again.

Only to pull his head back as another rifle shot passed so close he could feel the heat of the bullet.

"Damn, I still can't see that guy."

He discovered he was talking to no one. Morel had used him as covering fire and had disappeared.

I hope he doesn't run this time. His ass is on the line just as much as ours. We're dealing with pros here, not like those peasants and the two suits from the city.

Jacob scanned the jungle as rain continued to patter down. He saw a flicker of movement not far off to his left, but couldn't tell if it was Morel or a hostile.

The fire to their right had died down. He hoped Illary was all right. There was nothing he could do for her at the moment.

He glanced behind them. The underbrush grew thicker there.

"Jana," he whispered.

"Yeah," came a whisper back.

"We got to withdraw a little. Get out of this guy's line of sight. Crawl backwards, keeping your eye on the enemy. I'll cover you."

"OK."

Jacob reached out again without exposing his head, firing off a short burst before ducking to the other side of the tree and exposing just enough of his head to fire an aimed shot.

But not at that damn rifleman, whom he still couldn't see, but at two guys with shotguns advancing on his position.

They had already thrown themselves down after his unaimed burst, so he only managed to tag one of them before the rifleman fired again.

Jacob felt a sting in his shoulder and ducked back. Just a scratch, nicking the meat on his shoulder. Proved this guy was sharp, though, and Jacob still didn't have a chance to see where that fire had come from. Somewhere close ahead.

The more immediate problem was the guy about to rush his position.

Jacob pulled out a fragmentation grenade, yanked out the pin and, just as he heard a rustling sound close to his front, reached around the tree and lobbed the grenade at the approximate location.

Another rifle shot, but his hand moved back too quickly for the sniper.

A yell, then a detonation. Jacob hurried to the rear, running at a crouch and emptying his magazine at the underbrush.

The sniper didn't fire. He had probably put his head down for fear of more grenades.

Or out of the horror of what a frag grenade does to a man's body when it explodes close to him.

Jacob could hear the guy. He wasn't screaming. He wasn't moaning. It was more like the mewing of a cat—high-pitched, plaintive, weakening into silence after only a few seconds.

He tucked into a roll and got deep into the thicket. Off in the direction where Morel had disappeared there was a sharp cry, then nothing.

Jacob peered around and saw Jana's eyes peering out at him through a cluster of ferns. A couple of thick roots ran in front of and between her and him, offering a bit of protection. She edged along behind these to get closer to Jacob.

"The sniper is between the tree that forks about thirty yards ahead of us," she whispered. "But not right behind. He's standing behind a thinner tree you can see just between the fork."

Jacob dared a peek. He saw the tree she mentioned. Its thick trunk split into two about three feet from the ground, splaying wide so it could send up a broader leaf cover to capture as much sunlight as possible on its upper branches. Between these two, another ten yards on, stood a younger, thinner tree.

Jacob put his head back down, wishing he hadn't left his rifle with his pack back at the archaeologists' camp.

"The guy doesn't have much of a range of vision," Jacob whispered, "but sitting where we are, he's got us dead to rights."

"You go left and I'll go right. Maybe we'll meet up with the others."

Assuming Morel is still to the left.

Jacob decided to keep his doubts to himself, nodded, and withdrew a little more before shifting to the left. He snapped a fresh magazine into his MP5 and felt another twinge of pain in his bad wrist. Adrenaline had kept him from feeling it for the first part of the firefight, but he knew, after falling from that tree, that he could no longer trust it. He could tell his aim was off.

And where the hell was Morel, or the one or more guys who had been trying to flank them to their left?

The light was dying quickly now. They had to end this soon, or the enemy would get away, only to come back and hit them after darkness, where they'd have all the advantage of being familiar with the terrain.

Jacob darted from tree trunk to tree trunk, peering through the dimming light of the jungle. All he heard was the patter of rain.

He tried to pick up speed. That sniper would soon realize they had moved and shift position.

A body in camo lay in his path, his throat slit.

Nice one, Morel.

Jacob had angled to the left enough and now started moving forward, only to find another body with its throat slit.

A single shotgun blast thudded far to the right. Jana taking out an enemy, or the enemy taking out her?

He couldn't worry about that now. He had to find that sniper.

Instead, the sniper found him.

From his left rear came a shot that hummed past his ear and whickered through the brush. The blam of a shotgun sounded an instant later, followed by a cry and a thud.

Jacob ducked and rushed the sniper's position.

Morel had gotten there first. He stood over the man, who lay arms splayed, his chest a red ruin, his hunting rifle with scope just out of reach.

"Thanks. He almost got me," Jacob said. He looked around. "You think he was the last?"

"I think so."

The man moaned and shifted his foot. Jacob nudged him with his boot.

"Hey, muchacho. Who are you guys with?"

The man looked up at him with eyes clouded with pain.

"We … " He paused, as if remembering himself.

"You talk, and I'll patch you up," Jacob said.

The man struggled for a moment, then opened his mouth.

"There!" Morel whispered, crouching and pointing his shotgun.

Jacob turned to face this new threat, but instead heard a shotgun blast close by his head. He jumped to the side and looked at Morel.

He had shot the prisoner.

"He made a move," Morel said.

Jacob looked back where Morel had indicated.

"Sorry, my friend. A trick of the light. I can barely see in this murk."

"Damn it, he could have cleared this whole mess up!" Jacob fumed.

"He would have made a mess out of you."

"Jacob," came a call from beyond his line of sight. Jana's voice.

"Come here, we won't fire," he replied.

At least I won't. I can't say the same for this trigger-happy idiot.

Jana and Illary appeared out of the brush. Both looked unscathed.

"I think we cleared out them all," Illary said.

"We haven't seen any more over here," Jacob replied, casting Morel a contemptuous glance.

"Good," Jana said, letting out a long sigh. She looked worn out, and was still grieving her colleague.

"I think these were the guys who killed your friend," Jacob said. *For what little that helps.*

"Probably," Jana said. "But what about the guys you ran from yesterday? And the narcos? And those Americans on the boat? It seems like a whole lot of people are interested in this place."

"We should avoid them," Morel said. "This was a search and rescue and it failed. We killed the main suspects. I think we should get out while we can."

"We need to make camp soon," Illary said. "I suggest we get at least a kilometer into the jungle, well away from here so anyone else coming to this site won't find us. We'll post watches and break camp before sunrise. Get back to the river if we can."

"No!" Jana objected. "We have to go on, find that site Nasby was so interested in. It's what all these people are after, I'm sure of it. Let's do it your way, but instead of going to the river, we go find that site."

"Not a bad plan," Jacob said, "but I got a better idea. It won't be as comfortable, and it sure won't be as safe, but it will probably stop a lot of headaches in the long run."

"And what is that?" Illary asked.

Jacob grimaced. "You aren't going to like it, but I think it's the best way forward."

CHAPTER NINETEEN

El Teniente did not like this situation. The jungle was dark and quiet, expectant. As he peered through the murk, lit up here and there by ghostly shafts of moonlight, he sensed it held even more dangers than usual.

Their tribal guide had led them deep through the jungle in order to avoid the government officials who had just arrived in the area. While he felt confident they could take a bunch of *paisanos* and a pair of city boys, he didn't want the trouble, not from the government, and not from anyone else within earshot. It seemed like everyone was suddenly coming to this patch of jungle looking for El Dorado.

Although he had to thank that other group. It was one of the peasants he had captured and tortured who had told him all about the two officials taking a "vacation" from their bureaucratic jobs in Lima and hiring them to go hunt for the gold. The man was vague as to how the officials had discovered what the archaeologists were doing. They were connected to the antiquities department, so perhaps one of the gringos had said too much when getting the excavation permits.

And somehow, that loose talk got to another group, a deadlier group, who killed the gringos a few days ago.

Ever since, he had been torn between two jobs—scouting the jungle to try and find out what was going on, and waiting for a shipment of cocaine. El Teniente was only an officer in a vast army of narcotraffickers. He couldn't sneak away to do some other task and leave the shipment to be late. He would end up as dead as that peasant they had tortured.

But he had learned two things by spying on the government group and the group that had killed the archaeologist, who seemed to be mercenaries—the mercenaries hadn't found El Dorado for some reason, and they had called in reinforcements.

Those reinforcements, a bunch of gringos who came by boat, had made it to El Teniente's base just minutes after he had evacuated.

Things were getting all too confusing. This new group of gringos didn't seem to have any connection with the group of three gringos guided by a Quechua woman who had slaughtered some of his men. He had sworn vengeance, and now that his *kancha* was compromised, he had an excuse to get out of there, wreak vengeance on those four, and see what was going on with El Dorado.

It seemed like everyone wanted to find it and no one knew precisely where to look. The government group was way off, that was for sure. Typical.

So La Fantasma had taken them through jungle known to no one but his tribe, well away from any paths. It had been a hard, brutal march, but it had been a safe one. Night had fallen, the jungle had become nearly pitch-black, and yet La Fantasma had moved with an unerring confidence and led them right to their goal.

Now they approached the camp where the gringo archaeologists had been killed. La Fantasma had scouted the area as they had waited, a tense group of eight men all armed and ready. The tribesman had come back to say no one was there.

The rain had let up, the clouds had broken, and they advanced on the camp from the south under the light of a full moon that made the jungle an eerie patchwork of silver and black. They split up and skirted the path on either side, just in case.

El Teniente gripped his Ultimax machine gun, ready to mow down anyone unfamiliar. The tribesman walked a bit in front and to his left. He could just see the path as a silvery line through gaps in the shrubbery to his right. He could not hear or see the five men on the other side of the path. Good. They were being quiet and they were being careful. They had not fought off the other cartels and carved out a name for themselves in the drug trade without being so.

Which was why it came as such a surprise when an explosion tore through the jungle right where those men should be.

El Teniente threw himself on the ground, and that saved his life.

The ringing in his ears was not enough to drown out the snap of a rifle. The man behind him spun and fell. Before El Teniente could ready his machine gun, he saw the flare of the rifle a second time, and a second man fell.

La Fantasma bolted, melting into the jungle and disappearing like a dream. El Teniente and the one man left opened up where they had seen the rifle flare. The man's AK-47 and his own machine gun blared, raking the jungle with bullets. They kept firing until they emptied their magazines, then snapped new ones into place.

Just as they did, the rifle barked again, from their left this time. Surely it couldn't be the same man? No one could move that quickly.

The narco with El Teniente cried out and fell. Swiveling his machine gun, the officer who was now without soldiers to lead opened up again.

But only for a moment. A bullet pierced his heart, his finger slipped from the trigger, and he crumpled to the forest floor, consciousness fading away.

The last thing El Teniente saw was a vision of ancient Incan gold, riches he had never known in life, and would never enjoy in death.

* * *

Jacob scanned the jungle from his hiding place deep in the shadows. He had timed it perfectly. He knew if anyone came at the camp from the south, the smart thing to do would be to have two wings of the advancing force on either side of the path, so he had set up a claymore with a trip wire on one side, and then positioned himself on the other, directly opposite a small, open patch of forest canopy where the other advancing flank would briefly be illuminated by the moonlight.

A good thing the clouds finally broke and gave him moonlight, otherwise he wouldn't have been able to take out so many.

They had almost gotten him anyway. If he hadn't shifted position, that guy with the machine gun from hell would have torn him apart.

There was only one loose end, perhaps two. That native guide had slipped away, and if there was rearguard, they had gotten away too.

He didn't think they'd come back, though, not after the ass kicking he'd handed out.

Jacob reloaded his rifle, his bad hand fumbling the bullets. Damn. Every time he used it, it got worse and worse. He didn't have much fight left in him.

He pulled out his pistol and fired once in the air, then two more shots close together.

It was a signal to the others for "all clear." Jacob was guarding the southern perimeter of the camp. Morel was to the east, Jana to the west, and Illary to the north. They had been standing vigil all night, without sleep, without rest, waiting for the enemy. He had convinced the others that if they didn't turn and fight on ground of their choosing, they were bound to get ambushed by one or more of the enemy groups. Better to get it over with.

116

The jungle reverted to silence. Jacob checked the glowing hands of his wristwatch before covering it up again with his sleeve. Sunrise in a few minutes.

They were in a bad spot. Four exhausted people, two without military training, trying to hold off a wide area with limited resources against an unknown number of enemies. At least he'd put Jana in the least likely position to get attacked. The enemy would have to circle around the entire camp in the dark to hit her. Illary's position was partially protected by some marshy ground, leaving her relatively safe too.

Once he had reloaded, Jacob shifted to another position, one he hadn't fired from. There he rested for a minute, struggling against the tug of sleep.

Fire erupted in Morel's sector. He could hear the Frenchmen firing with his MP5, and the thud of return rifle fire and the crack of an AK-47.

Jacob peered at the moonlit portions of the area to his front, on alert for another attack here. Perhaps what he had fought off had only been a probe and the real attack was what Morel faced.

The fire heated up, then he heard a hiss and an eerie red glow illuminated the jungle in that direction.

Morel had sent up a flare. A distress sign. Jacob couldn't directly see it because of the canopy, but the glow told him all he needed to know.

Morel had more than he could handle.

It had been agreed that Jacob would be the mobile unit and that Jana and Illary would stay put. They couldn't be risked as much. The mission needed Jana's archaeological knowledge and Illary's jungle expertise more than it needed either of the two men.

Giving a last searching look to his front and not seeing any enemy, Jacob made a beeline for Morel's sector. Already the moon was setting, its glow dimming in the forest, but in contrast the sun was lightening the eastern horizon, turning the black sky blue. It was still dim in the jungle, offering plenty of places to hide, but there was just enough light for Jacob's sharp eyes to see by.

The firing told him the direction. It was increasing in tempo. It sounded like the Frenchman faced every single one of those guys they had spotted back at the ruins. Morel really was having a tough time of it.

Something caught on Jacob's foot and he fell, only just managing to turn himself and land on his shoulder and not his bad wrist.

A creeper. He pulled his foot out from under it and tested his ankle. It throbbed, but still moved when he told it to. The shooting continued.

Damn, that was a rookie move. I'm more worn out than I thought.

Jacob rose, holding onto a nearby tree for support. He eased weight onto his twisted ankle and found it could support him with a minimum of protest. Good, he hadn't sprained it. The pain he felt was just the initial twinge of a twist. He could ignore it like he could ignore all the insect bites and bumps and bruises he'd gotten on this mission and the last.

The trip showed him he couldn't ignore his fatigue, though. The pain in his wrist demanded attention too.

He moved through the jungle again, looking as much at his feet as the area around him. The sky gradually grew brighter, but not bright enough to fully illuminate his way. This dim world of shadows and obstacles was the perfect place to fight a defensive action. He and Morel had the advantage.

He hoped. When he had spied on the Peruvian peasants working for those two government guys, he noted how confident they appeared in the jungle. They had probably been picked because they had experience as hunters.

That would probably explain why the claymore Morel had set up hadn't gone off. The peasants had spotted it. It was only pure luck that Jacob's claymore had gone off. If that native hunter had been on the other side of the path, he would have detected the tripwire for sure.

Well, Jacob was a hunter too. He'd hunted terrorists in the jungles of Burma and the Philippines, and elk and bear with Aaron Peters in northern Canada.

The firing was close now, focused on his front left. Maybe thirty, forty yards away.

Jacob froze, then melted into the shadow of a thick tree.

The fight was closer than he thought. He saw two shadows moving stealthily through the underbrush just ahead of him and heading in the same direction.

He's been flanked. Bound to happen when you're outnumbered twenty to one.

Jacob raised his MP5, thought better of it, and slung it across his back. Instead, he drew his 9mm automatic with his left hand. He'd give his injured right hand a break until he truly needed it.

118

In the couple of seconds it took to do this, the figures had vanished into the gloom. Jacob angled a bit to the left, alert for any more creepers or roots that might trip him up. At each tree he paused to look around.

His caution got rewarded when he saw two more figures following the first pair, just a few yards behind.

Jacob angled further away to ensure he remained out of sight, then picked up the pace as much as he dared. Once he felt he had gotten ahead of the first pair, he cut sharply to the right …

… and nearly stumbled over the two leading Peruvians crouched in a thicket of ferns.

Two quick shots took them out, and then Jacob had to fling himself on the ground as the second pair opened fire from far closer than he anticipated them to be.

CHAPTER TWENTY

Jana grew increasingly impatient at the sounds of battle first in Jacob's sector, then Morel's. She had been hiding in a dense bit of bush, monitoring a clearer area up the slope to the north of the camp, ever since sunset. She'd been tortured by insects and lack of sleep for hours, but even more than that she was tortured by the mysterious words on that slip of paper she had discovered from Nasby's notebook.

... through the cleft at local sunrise the beams shine down on the entrance, invisible otherwise. How great, how brilliant the Incans were! To use the natural topography so cleverly, to find connections in the natural world to help them in the material one. They ...

If only more of the page had been preserved! Without context, Nasby's words meant nothing.

She stared out from her hiding place behind the twisting roots of a large tree. The trail she had briefly followed the previous day went up the gentle slope and spread out into several smaller, fainter trails. It looked like the team had been systematically searching the area. She could see the trees thinning out in that direction, and the vague outline of a large rock outcropping about a kilometer away.

The sky was brightening with dawn, and soon the top of that outcropping would get illuminated with light. It would take some time before the sun rose enough for it to shine its rays on the jungle. There would be poor visibility for fighting for at least half an hour more.

Jana jerked with a sudden thought, all fatigue suddenly vanished.

The sun hits the top of that rock first. Then hits the jungle as it rises.

That's what Nasby meant by local sunrise.

And the cleft he mentioned. Outcroppings such as that are often seriously weathered and have split tops. I bet if I could see better I'd spot a cleft in that outcropping.

Jana realized she had stood up. Firing continued in Morel's sector. She was insane to stand. What if another thrust came at her position?

Unlikely. That's why Jacob had posted her here. Illary's swampy side of the camp wasn't going to see much action, either.

She shifted to the right, trying to keep under cover while at the same time trying get a better view of that outcropping. She hadn't ventured much further up the slope than this, and hadn't taken any special note of the outcropping except to see the jungle petered out beyond it, obviously giving way to a rockier and hillier area that remained out of sight.

Jana kept searching for another few seconds as gunfire crackled in the jungle behind her, and a chance break in the foliage showed her what she wanted to see.

A clear view of the top of the outcropping. It was about two hundred feet tall, tapering up to a narrow summit, which was cut with a vertical cleft running right through the middle.

Jana's heart nearly stopped with excitement.

Now she knew where the real mission lay.

But she couldn't do it alone. Not even with the promise of a great discovery dangling before her.

She sprinted for Illary's position, stumbled over a vine, righted herself, and kept going.

As she neared the Quechua woman's sector, she slowed. She wasn't entirely sure where Illary had positioned herself. The fire in Morel's area began to die down. Knowing Morel's abilities, the initial assault had no doubt suffered heavy losses, and now the survivors had grown careful, firing from carefully chosen spots or creeping through the still-dim jungle, searching for prey.

She passing through some bushes, keeping low so as not to expose her head.

After a few paces, she stopped dead, the cold of a muzzle pressed to the back of her head.

"Jesus," Illary whispered. "You scared the hell out of me."

"Look who's talking," Jana said after her heart decided to resume beating.

"What are you doing here?"

"I figured out that slip of paper from Nasby's notebook. There's an outcropping of rock just to the west of here with a cleft on it. When the sun hits it, I think it shines through to reveal a hidden cave entrance."

Even in the dim lights, Jana could see Illary's eyes widen with excitement. "My ancestors did a lot with the light of the sun and moon. They were great astronomers, like the Maya in Mexico." A gunshot in Morel's sector cut her short. "But this isn't the time for archaeological investigation."

"But it is! Everyone coming here isn't really going for the camp, they want to find what Nasby and his team were searching for. If they have gathered any clues, like more scraps from the notebook, they'll be heading there, not here."

"But they're attacking here."

"One group is, or at the most two. We seem to be facing three or four groups—the narcos, the government people, the Americans on the boat, and the people we fought here at the camp yesterday evening."

"You're right …" Illary looked in the direction of the fighting. "But to leave our posts, to leave them vulnerable … "

"If they circle around this way, they're heading for the outcropping and the hills beyond it. Also, we can only see the entrance to the cave if the morning sun is shining. We couldn't have spotted anything in yesterday's rain."

"We could wait until tomorrow morning and hope for another sunny day."

"Stay twenty-four hours in this bullet magnet? No, thank you. And we might be more vulnerable in the long run if one of these groups finds Nasby's discovery. They'll try to wipe out everyone in the area to keep it, and if they get away with whatever it is, they'll have gotten away with murder."

"You're talking like Nasby really did find El Dorado."

"Not really, not in a literal sense. But the artifacts we found in the tent are valuable enough on the international antiquities market. What if there's more? A lot more? What if there are a few gold artifacts too? That's why the narcos are after it. A couple of gold statuettes would be worth more than a drug shipment."

"I see your point, but … "

She looked again toward Morel's position. The firing had died down completely, replaced with an ominous silence.

"We need to go," Jana said. "I need you to come with me. I can't navigate this jungle alone without risking getting lost."

"Let's go check out the situation with them first. We can go together."

"There's no time. The sun is going to hit that cleft in a matter of minutes. If we don't see the spot where it beams through, we won't find the cave. That's what Nasby's notebook implies. Because as the sun rises, the beam will move to a different spot."

"Like sunrise on the Intihuatana Stone," Illary murmured. She nodded. "All right, but let's hurry."

122

Jana squeezed her shoulder. "Thank you."

Illary grinned. "Girls got to stick together."

"The only thing sticking to me at the moment are about two hundred insects."

"Maybe they're girls too. Let's go."

They withdrew from Illary's position and returned to Jana's. From there they scanned the slope ahead, saw no obvious threats, and moved uphill. They passed through a few more thickets growing in the increasingly stony ground amid fewer and smaller trees.

It wasn't long before they could see the rock outcropping clearly, and beyond that a rising series of foothills, and beyond that, the mountains. The sky was a pale blue now, and the rising sun shone off the tops of some of the closest and lowest foothills.

"Just in time," Jana panted. They were running now, all caution gone in the excitement.

They came to the outcropping, part of a low hill made up of a different and harder stone than that surrounding it, which got isolated as the softer stone weathered away on all sides to leave this strange peak.

Nasby was right. The Incas were brilliant to spot this natural bit of terrain and use it to their advantage.

They skirted the spire's scrabbly base and worked their way around to the other side. Just beyond they could see a deeply eroded, almost vertical stone slope on the side of a high hill. Erosion from heavy rainfall had seamed it with countless deep vertical fissures, like wrinkles on a wizened old face. The sun was just touching its grassy summit.

Jana and Illary ran around to the far side of the spire and stopped. They hadn't heard any gunshots for several minutes, but even in their anticipation of the beam of light that was just now lowering down the lip of the cliff, they checked around them.

No one else was in sight. While they knew they were probably still in danger, for the moment they had this wondrous vision for themselves.

Directly above them, a thin beam of light shot through the crevasse at the middle of the spire, shining a bright circle on the face of the cliff. It moved slowly downward like a spotlight.

Jana and Illary stood in silence. For the moment, even the birds and insects remained still. The rational part of Jana's mind knew they had gone quiet because of the gunfight, scared like all jungle denizens of strange sounds that might be predators. In her heart, however, she felt that they were showing reverence for the magical sight they all were now witnessing.

The spot of light continued to slide down the cliff. When it got about two-thirds of the way to the bottom, and the surrounding countryside grew ever lighter from the rising sun, the shaft of light illuminated a narrow crevasse in the face of the cliff. Until the light hit it, the spot looked like a thousand other shadows in that deeply seamed rockface.

But with that shaft of light upon it, a tunnel barely five feet high and a little more than a foot wide became clearly visible running into the cliff.

Jana took in a deep breath, eyes going wide. It felt like when she first uncovered that Roman mosaic in Morocco, or when she and Jacob discovered hidden chambers in the catacombs outside Alexandria, or when she and Jacob found the secret tunnels beneath the Dome of the Rock, or when she and Jacob discovered an almost perfectly preserved pirate ship.

This promised just as much as those great discoveries.

She and Illary had both started to walk forward. Illary was repeating something under her breath in Quechua. Jana didn't know the words, but it sounded like a prayer.

They reached the base of the hill just as the beam of light came to the base, then diffused and was gone as the sun passed above the spire of rock to shine all over the landscape.

Local sunrise.

Eyes fixed on the spot the beam had revealed, they walked slowly up the slope. Without the direct ray of the sun, the entrance had disappeared, just another shadow in the rough face of the cliff. It didn't matter. They knew the spot now. A faint trail of footprints helped lead their way, the last steps of Professor Carstairs Nasby and his crew.

The insects and birds remained still. The two women said nothing. The only sound was their footsteps on the gritty earth.

And then it stood before them, a thin slit in the cliff like a half-open door. They could see a passageway sloping downward, disappearing into the Stygian gloom.

"Let's go down there," Jana said, her voice coming out hushed with excitement.

"All right," Illary replied, sounding no less enthralled. "You got your flashlight?"

"Yeah."

They pulled them out.

"Wait!"

Jacob's voice called from behind them. They turned to see him sprinting around the base of the spire, limping slightly.

"Jacob! What's going on?" Jana asked.

"I fought off the narcos," he said breathlessly as he approached, "then the Peruvian government group hit Morel's side. When I went to help I nearly got bushwhacked by a couple I didn't spot but managed to take them out. We fought the rest them off and with the sunrise decided to join you. Then I saw the sunlight hitting the top of this split spire and realized that the sunlight might shine through there to illuminate a cave entrance, just like your friend said in his notebook."

He got to them and stopped, panting. "And so here I am."

"You figured that out all by yourself?" Jana asked.

He grinned. "Sure. I'm an archaeologist now."

"Where's Morel?" Illary asked.

"Patrolling the perimeter. Let's check out this cave. After that, we need to go fetch our packs from where we hid them and get out of here."

Illary nodded. "All right. Let's go and—"

Her sentence was cut off by the crack of an AK-47. Blood burst from her head, and then she slammed into the cliff wall and sank to the ground.

CHAPTER TWENTY ONE

Jacob grabbed Jana as she screamed and pulled her inside the cave as more shots came from the Kalashnikov. He didn't have time to spot the shooter, but knew another group had gotten in on the game.

Bullets smacked off the sides of the narrow cleft in the rock. One ricocheted inside the tunnel and Jacob felt a tug at his belt and a sudden wetness. He looked down and saw his canteen had been pierced, the water pouring down his leg.

At least it wasn't blood, like what covered the face of poor Illary who lay dead at the cave entrance.

More shots rang out. Jacob and Jana penetrated further into the gloom. Jana switched on her flashlight and they found themselves in a narrow corridor, what looked like a natural crevasse that had been widened and shaped in part by human hands. It was too narrow to go together, and barely wide enough to walk facing forward. Jacob led with Jana slightly behind.

The archaeologist stopped. "Aren't we going to fight?"

"It's a bad position," Jacob said. "Only one of us can fire while a bunch of them can shoot from various angles at us. Plus, even if they don't hit us, the ricochets will. Look at my canteen."

He turned on his own flashlight and shone it on himself.

Jana looked down and saw what he meant. "Damn. But we have to fight back! We have to avenge Illary."

"We will," Jacob reassured her. "But we'll do it smart. We'll see where this leads and set up an ambush for them. They'll have to come down with their lights on We'll have ours off."

In the glow of his flashlight, Jana's face suddenly turned harsh, like an avenging fury.

"All right. And with this shotgun at such close quarters I can take out two of the bastards at a time."

Jacob felt a sudden tug of regret. *What am I creating here?*

"Come on," he said, pulling at her hand.

The tunnel descended, turning slightly so the last bit of sunlight was soon snuffed out. After a few more yards in the narrow tunnel, which grew a bit higher but not wider, Jacob stopped.

"Let's turn off our flashlights for a minute and see if they're following," he whispered.

They did, and were plunged into utter darkness. They waited a minute as their eyes adjusted, and found the darkness wasn't complete. A faint shine, or more the hint of light, emanated from the direction from which they had come. The bright sunlight of the Peruvian Amazon sent its last feeble rays, scattered and diminished, deep into this tunnel to make the shadows the barest shade lighter than black.

It was not enough to see by. Jacob couldn't even see the figure of the woman standing right next to him.

He could hear her, though. She was crying softly to herself.

Jacob realize he still held her hand. He squeezed it.

He wanted to say something reassuring, but he didn't dare speak in case someone else was down here, lights off, listening.

Jana snuffled and he heard her wiping her eyes with her free hand. He kept squeezing the other one.

She squeezed back.

"Let's go," she whispered.

He turned on his flashlight, blinking at the sudden light after such profound darkness. Jana turned on hers as well. They continued down, the tunnel becoming straighter and leveling out.

Then they came to a wider section, obviously worked out from the natural fissure. The roughness of the original stone could be seen on the ceiling ten feet above their heads, but the walls, now a little more than a yard apart, had been smoothed to a flat surface.

At head level were several strange lines scratched into the surface. They consisted of a crescent-shaped line bending downward, and descending from these were dozens of other lines splaying out like rays from the sun in a child's drawing. Each of the vertical lines had several pecked dots or loops at various points along their length.

Jacob looked around and saw dozens of these strange drawings all along both walls. While similar, each had a different number of lines, and different patterns of dots and loops on the lines.

"*Quipu*," Jana whispered.

"What?"

"I think these are representations of *quipu*. The Inca didn't have a writing system, but they could record numbers and some basic words using a system of strings tied to a central cord. The strings would have different types of knots set at different points on the string. Each type of knot and its position signified something different, either a number

127

or a word for a type of object. They used them for trade and census data. I've never seen them carved into a wall like this before."

"Why not make up a proper writing system like the Maya?"

"Nobody knows. It was such a big empire you'd think they would. Some people say that because the empire stretched so far, almost the length of the west coast of South America, it encompassed too many languages. A writing system based on the Incan language would be a lot of trouble for local ethnic groups, but learning the *quipu* system would be much easier for everyone, since it only included numbers and a basic vocabulary. That's just a theory, though. It's a mystery."

Jacob scanned the drawings. "So what do they say?"

"I don't know. I never learned to read them. Actually, no one fully understands them."

"Got a guess?"

Jana motioned toward the tunnel, which narrowed again a bit further on and ran beyond the reach of their flashlights.

"Maybe our answer lies down there."

They continued. Despite the danger, and his sadness and anger at seeing a good law enforcement agent gunned down before his eyes, Jacob felt a rising sense of excitement and anticipation. He had never had much more than a casual interest in the past, but his recent adventures with Jana had changed all that. The discoveries they had made together had opened up a new world to him, a world of ancient people and legendary figures, their deeds and ways of life. Now he understood why she had gone into archaeology. There was a thrill to discovering something that wasn't like any other experience.

He felt honored to be sharing that thrill with her.

They continued down the corridor. Jacob was dimly aware that they were still holding hands, but in the excitement of the moment he didn't question why.

The corridor continued. The air here was stale, with very little circulation to the surface.

"Wait," Jana said, tugging on his hand.

They stopped. Jana shone her flashlight on the floor.

A fine covering of dust showed numerous booted prints.

Jacob let go of Jana's hand and readied his submachine gun. He peered down the corridor but didn't see anyone.

"I think it was Nasby and his crew," Jana said. "They found this place. That would explain the artifacts back at camp. At the main hallway with the *quipu* engravings, I noticed some circular marks on the dust on the floor. I think that was from the pots they retrieved."

A faint echo made them stop talking and switch off their lights. Once again, darkness fell over them.

They waited. The sound came again, too faint to determine its origin. But they did see the faintest of lights. It couldn't be sunlight, not this deep down and after so many twists and turns of the corridor.

Someone else was in here.

CHAPTER TWENTY TWO

Jana gripped her shotgun tight, peering at the faint light as it slowly grew. Again she heard a distant sound. Footsteps? She couldn't say. She had no doubt, though, that they were no longer alone.

A ghostly cry came echoing down the darkened corridor to them.

"Jacob! Jana!"

Jana shuddered from superstitious fear, imagining the ghosts of vengeful Incas.

Half a second later reason took over, and she realized it could only be one person.

The next call confirmed it.

"Jacob! Jana! It's me, Gaspard Morel! Are you down there?"

Jana called out, "Yes, we're here! There are no side corridors. Just follow the tunnel down."

They moved back to the main chamber to meet him, and arrived at the same time. He looked flushed, excited.

"I killed a couple of the narcos you missed," he told Jacob. "They were the ones who killed Illary."

Jacob only nodded, his face growing stony. Morel went on.

"Don't feel bad, my friend. I think they didn't come to your sector but were rather working their way around to come at us from another direction. Then they lay low while we battled the Peruvian government force."

"It's no official government force, not if they're arming peasants," Jana said.

"No, the government is better off without them." Morel let out a little chuckle.

Anger rose up in her. *How can you laugh when Illary is dead?*

"You sure the area is clear?" Jacob asked.

"As sure as I can be," Morel said with a shrug. "No one saw me come in here, at least."

Jana turned away. "Let's go see where this tunnel leads."

"What are these carvings on the wall?" the Frenchman asked.

"An old Inca form of record keeping. I can't read it," Jana said without stopping.

130

They retraced their steps and continued down the tunnel. Morel kept up a constant chatter, asking about everything they were seeing, about the Incas, and about Nasby's research. Jana grew increasingly annoyed. She was still stunned by what had happened to Illary and didn't need this guy jabbering away. He hadn't shown this much interest during the entire trip.

Jacob put a stop to it.

"Keep quiet, buddy. We need to hear if anyone else comes in here."

"I cleared the area."

"That's impossible to know for sure. A million narcos and mercenaries could hide in that jungle."

"Whatever you say," Morel grumbled.

They continued down a narrow tunnel single file, with Jana in the front, Jacob behind her, and Morel taking up the rear.

Once Jana thought she heard something behind them. She stopped, peering past the two men into the darkness beyond.

"Did you hear that?" she whispered.

"I didn't hear anything," Morel said.

"Let's turn our lights out."

They did, and the darkness this deep into the tunnel was total. It gave Jana the chills, while in another way reassuring her. No one else was shining any lights in here.

Still, they waited a full minute before turning their flashlights back on and continuing down the corridor.

They didn't have far to go.

Their flashlights caught a yellowish gleam up ahead, which grew as they approached. Jana slowed, gasping with wonder.

The corridor widened into a small antechamber. At the far end stood a doorway, with small niches in the wall at head height to either side. Jana supposed they had once held statues now vanished.

But the larger room beyond wasn't empty.

She stopped in her tracks, staring in wonder.

The room was piled high with gold objects—plates, goblets, statuettes, all of Inca manufacture. As she looked more closely, she saw the goblets were filled with earrings and rings and gold nuggets. One nugget was the size of her fist.

And there was more, much more. A gold breastplate for the king, gold crown topped with a feather headdress. Figurines of llamas and jaguars. Elaborate face masks. As the three explorers focused their lights on the heap of treasure, their eyes were dazzled by its brilliance, its sheer worth, and its groundbreaking historical significance.

"El Dorado," Morel whispered. "It's really real. I never really believed it until now."

"Neither did I," Jana said, still staring. "No archaeologist did. Oh, we hoped that the Incas had hidden some of their treasure somewhere, but we never dreamed we'd actually be so lucky as to find it."

"And your friend did," Jacob said.

Jana nodded. Such a shame Nasby died at the moment of his triumph, but at least for a few precious hours, he felt an archaeologist's greatest sense of accomplishment since the discovery of the tomb of Tutankhamun.

Morel stepped forward.

"Don't touch anything!" Jana said. "This is an archaeological site."

"It's also a battlefield," Jacob said, looking back the way they had come. "We should secure this place, hide the entrance somehow, and then report it to the proper authorities."

Morel stood at the edge of the gold heap, studying everything.

"Ah!"

He plucked up an idol. While it wasn't the largest of the items, or the most aesthetically pleasing, it was distinct from the rest.

It showed a man with a skull for a face, a mouthful of fangs, and a pair of twisted horns. Its eyes were blood red gemstones.

Morel held it up. "Supay, god of the dead. He rules over the underworld, and has the power of life and death over all humanity."

Jana blinked. "Wait. How do you know that?"

Morel smiled and tucked the figurine into the pocket of his vest. Jana was about to object when he leveled his MP5 at them.

Jana sucked in her breath. Jacob remained impassive.

"Put down your weapons," Morel ordered.

Slowly, they obeyed.

"Now your pistols. Carefully. Correctly. With two fingers, others spread wide."

They obeyed. Jana pulled her pistol from its holster with her thumb and forefinger. It slipped from her trembling hand and clattered on the stone floor, making her jump.

Morel chuckled. He hadn't moved an inch. "If you think that will distract me, you are mistaken."

"It slipped."

"It doesn't matter."

They were both disarmed now. As much as they could be. Jacob was deadly in unarmed combat and she wasn't too bad herself.

But they stood on the wrong end of a submachine gun and Morel's finger was on the trigger.

She had seen him fight. He was almost as good as Jacob. Tricks wouldn't work. Rushing him wouldn't work.

"Why?" was all Jana could ask. "Do you really think you can get away with all this gold?"

"Sure we can!" an American voice sounded behind them.

Suddenly the corridor lit up with half a dozen lights. It was the crew of mercenaries posing as fishermen they had tangled with on the river. All had rifles pointing in their direction.

"You got it?" one of them asked Morel.

"I do."

"What the hell?" Jacob bellowed. "You were with them the entire time?"

Morel chuckled. "Yes, my friend. We did not intend on bumping into each other on the river, but I played my part well, no? And during that gunfight, you were too busy to notice that all my shots deliberately missed. We were working with the Peruvian mercenaries we killed at camp yesterday. My shots didn't go wide that time. No, you see, they needed to be punished. It was they who killed the archaeologists, but they were thugs, and stupid, and made too many mistakes. They were supposed to take Professor Nasby hostage, but when he killed one of their number, they shot before thinking and killed him. Then in their rage they burned the bodies and trashed the camp. The fools burnt the notebooks! Then they didn't know where to find El Dorado. But fate played into our hands. A scrap of paper told Jana all she needed to know to solve the puzzle, and here we are."

"So this was all planned beforehand?" Jana still couldn't believe it.

"Yes, but things didn't go as expected. I was only supposed to be the middleman, using my police connections to help smuggle the items out of the country. But when our Peruvian friends got trigger happy, and Nasby managed to radio a distress call, I had to take on a more central role."

"But how did you even know what they were looking for?"

Morel patted the pocket with the figurine. Its skull face and horns stuck out of the top like some Satanic jack-in-the-box.

"A certain millionaire occultist has been studying the legends of El Dorado for many years. He actually worships the ancient Incan gods.

Bizarre, no? Few know of his strange religion. Most know him as a rich benefactor of excavations in South America. He bankrolled Nasby's expedition."

"And he knew Nasby would never consent to this, and so he had him killed," Jana growled, hands balling into fists. "Wait, you shot Illary, didn't you? Using an AK you picked up so we would think it was someone else."

Morel shrugged. "I wanted to get all of you, but you were too quick. As for my patron, the man is crazy, I'll admit. You know he thinks this little statue will give him the power over life and death? I've seen his mansion in Buenos Aires. It has rooms that look like something out of a horror film. Skeletons and pentagrams and mummified babies. The man is a freak, but a rich freak. If we could get him this statue, he promised us the rest of the treasure."

"And it will make us all multimillionaires," one of the Americans said.

They moved forward.

"We'll each have more than we'll ever be able to spend," another of the fake fishermen said. "Morel, kill these idiots and let's get loading this stuff up."

Morel grinned, aimed his MP5 at Jana's chest, and pulled the trigger.

CHAPTER TWENTY THREE

Jacob coiled to spring. Morel pulled the trigger, and his submachine gun, instead of sending a burst of bullets tearing through Jana's body, did nothing except make a soft click.

That's because back in the jungle, Jacob had disabled it while Morel was distracted. Luckily, the corrupt cop hadn't checked it or tried to use it since then.

Jacob leapt on him. The Frenchman was so surprised he didn't even fight back as Jacob flipped him, sending him flying into the bunched-up American mercenaries.

They fell like bowling pins.

It would have been comical if Jacob wasn't fighting for his life.

He snatched up his own MP5 at the same instant Jana grabbed her shotgun. They fired at the mass of men trying to untangle themselves.

It was a slaughter. Jacob sprayed them on full auto while Jana blammed away with her shotgun, pumping the action and then pulling the trigger as fast as she could. The gunshots were deafening in such close quarters. Jacob's wrist ached and his aim was off, but it was impossible to miss at such close range. The men cried out, flailed on the floor, tried to scramble away.

It was hopeless. Soon all lay on the ground, their bodies savaged by several wounds each.

No, not all. Jacob scanned the bloody heap of bodies and saw Morel's was not among them, and the crew of that riverboat had included at least two more men than he saw here.

"Get behind the doorway!" Jacob shouted, leaping to one side. He could barely hear himself through the ringing in his ears.

Jana must have figured out what he meant, because she bolted for the cover of the opposite side of the doorway.

Just in time. A burst from an AK-47 tore through the air just between them, the bullets panging off the priceless relics in the treasury behind them.

Jana looked at him from the opposite side of the antechamber as she fed fresh shells into the back of her shotgun. He waited until she was loaded up before removing the magazine from his MP5 and replacing it with a full one. Blood ran from the heap of bodies just around the corner, slowly covering the floor of the room in a widening pool, as if eager to touch the gold on the other side.

He and Jana were stuck. No way could they get out of this room without getting shot. The corridor was too narrow and there were no places to hide. They would be sitting ducks just like those poor bastards bleeding out at their feet.

Of course, Morel and his buddies couldn't advance either.

Jacob had never fully trusted the guy after he killed his first prisoner, and then didn't trust him at all after he killed the second. The world was full of corrupt cops, and Jacob had gotten an increasingly bad feeling about him. His mistakes in combat began to look deliberate.

Even so, Jacob had been unsure of himself when he disabled Morel's weapon and refused to share his grenades when the Interpol officer asked for a couple. Turned out to be the right choice on both counts.

Jacob pulled out his last flashbang grenade. He had a couple of fragmentation grenades too, but he didn't know how much stress the walls and roof could take. He held it up. Jana nodded, shrank back into the corner, plugged her ears with her fingers, and shut her eyes.

Jacob shut his eyes too as he tossed it as far as he could down the hallway.

It went off with an ear-splitting roar, magnified by the narrow tunnel. Jacob staggered back, momentarily stunned even though he had been around the corner. He opened his eyes and found himself leaning against the wall in a daze. The world spun around him and he barely managed to remain on his feet.

For a second he remained there, trying to pull himself together.

Jana got it together first. She was less worn out. She staggered to the corner and fired off three blasts from her shotgun in rapid succession.

Jacob recovered enough to peek around the corner too.

He saw nothing. There were no bodies in the corridor past the ones they had mown down at the entrance to the antechamber.

Morel and the others had fled.

Jacob turned off his flashlight. Jana did the same. They saw a dwindling light fading beyond the nearest turn of the hallway.

He stumbled past the open doorway to join up with Jana.

"We have to go after them!" she told him.

The way Jana's mouth contorted, he could tell she was yelling, but he could barely hear her. The firing, followed by the grenade, had all but deafened them.

At least Morel and the others would be affected too, but they had been further away. Their hearing might not be as bad, and they would recover quicker.

They needed to follow them now.

But if those guys laid a trap for them, they'd have no place to dive for cover.

They had to risk it. Keeping a close eye on the corridor, Jacob picked his way through the bodies. He gave each a quick pat-down, checking for grenades. He found none. He wiped his bloody hand on a clean section of one of their shirts and moved a bit down the hallway.

Jana joined him. She put a finger to her lips, then turned off her flashlight. Jacob still had his on. He pointed down the hallway and made walking motions with two of his fingers, then looked at her questioningly. She nodded.

Good idea. We keep in the dark and they might not see or hear us coming.

He switched off his light and began to walk with uncertain steps down the hallway. He had to touch both walls with his hands, leaving his MP5 to dangle by its strap. A bad situation with no other options. It was so dark here he'd keep bumping into the wall otherwise.

Jana kept close behind him. At least he hoped so. The ringing continued so loudly in his ears that he couldn't hear a thing. Up ahead, there shone the faintest hint of light.

He kept going. It was cool in here after the jungle, and Jana's warm breath on the back of his neck was a welcome contrast. She followed close behind him. He kept a steady pace, hoping she'd match it. He didn't want her to bump into him. Well, actually he did, but he didn't want to make any noise the enemy might hear.

Despite the crazy situation he found himself in, he couldn't help but wonder what she thought of him now. She had hated him for ripping her out of her old life, and for taking up so much of Aaron's time, but that conversation they had back at the camp made Jacob think they had formed a bond too.

Focus, idiot. You care about her? Then get her out of this alive.

But he couldn't stop thinking about it. Maybe it was because they were the last two on the mission. Maybe it was her proximity in the dark. Maybe he was simply cracking up.

His fingers lost touch with the wall. Jacob stopped in surprise and Jana bumped into him. He groped around and found they had passed through a doorway. For a heart-stopping second he thought they had ventured into some area they hadn't seen before and gotten lost in the darkness underground before he realized they had made it to the room with the carvings on the wall.

One of his searching hands touched Jana's. She held on to his and they angled to the left to reach the wall before slowly making their way along it to the door on the opposite side of the room.

They got to the door and paused. Jacob could see a faint glimmer of light up ahead. Sunlight? He tried to remember if they could see sunlight at this point. Tried and failed. The fight, the betrayal, and the disorientation of being in this dark underground space had confused his mind.

He stood still for a moment. Jana remained silent, holding his hand. He tried not to think about that and her warm breath on his cheek as he stared and listened. The ringing in his ears had lessened, but still interfered with his hearing.

The light did not change, and he heard no sound, or at least no sound loud enough to break through his temporary near-deafness.

Yeah, probably sunlight.

If those guys simply ran out of here, they're way ahead by now.

Nothing he could do about that. They had to proceed carefully if they wanted to get out of this place with their lives.

They continued their slow progress up the passageway, trailing their fingers along both walls.

Soon they didn't have to. The light grew brighter, and now Jacob felt sure it was sunlight. It illuminated the passageway enough that he could ready his gun and stalk forward, alert for any changes in the light that would signal someone else in the hallway up ahead.

The hallway sloped up more steeply now, and Jacob remembered this was the initial part. Almost there.

After a few more steps, the doorway came into view, a bright blue rectangle of sky.

No, not a perfect rectangle. There was a small rectangular shape poking into the lower left-hand corner.

Jacob paused, wondering what it was.

Then he it hit him.

A claymore. Morel took his claymore mine and set it up at the entrance.

Jacob got on his hands and knees and tried to see the tripwire. The contrast of the sunlight against his dark-adapted eyes made it difficult. He moved his head this way and that, trying to make it out. Jana had crouched down beside him, obviously having figured out the same thing. Smart woman. Detecting claymore tripwires had probably not been part of her teenage training, but you never knew with Aaron Peters.

Where is that damn thing?

Suddenly, a deafening blast and shockwave knocked him flat on his back. The corridor shook, something hard struck his head, and he knew no more.

CHAPTER TWENTY FOUR

Jana fell backwards, smacking her head against the stone floor. She cried out as something hit her in the stomach. The corridor filled with dust and falling debris, blinding her and making her cough. Another blow, to her shoulder this time, followed by a painful one to her shin.

She struggled into a sitting position, blinking and trying to orient herself. That bastard had set off a claymore at the entrance, which was now nearly blocked with debris. Morel hadn't aimed it down the corridor, but made the blast go against the wall to seal the tunnel. Through the remaining sunlight she could see more stones shearing off from the ceiling to crash on the floor below.

Jana was all but deaf now, and could not hear the crackling of ancient stone that she knew must resound inside the passageway.

She could feel it, though. This whole place would collapse in a couple more seconds.

That was Morel's intention. He knew Jacob was good enough that he might spot a tripwire, so he had set off the claymore remotely in order to bury them and the treasure. Then they could dig up the site at their leisure and retrieve the gold.

Jana got to her feet, then got knocked back on her knees by a stone hitting her shoulder. Jacob lay on the ground, covered in dust and small stones, a black spot on his dusty head from a stone that had struck him.

She touched his head and came away with blood on her hand.

Without even knowing if he was dead or alive, she grabbed him and dragged him toward the entrance.

A stone hit her on the head, too small to knock her out but big enough to send a spark of pain through her. Another hit her hand, cutting the back of it. Still she dragged her friend toward that beckoning and ever shrinking patch of sunlight.

The floor shook in a final convulsion. Jana hauled him up and over the heap of stones piled at the entrance and tumbled down the other side.

Praying the enemy wasn't there to shoot her as she emerged, she scrambled to her feet and grabbed Jacob, who lay slumped over the pile of stones.

Just as she wrenched him out to tumble on the hillside outside, there was a final shudder and a groan like a chorus of subterranean demons, and the entire tunnel collapsed. A spray of dust and stones spewed out of the entrance to push her back.

She ended up lying on the hillside, spitting out grit and rubbing her eyes.

For a second she could only lie there stunned, then the danger of her situation made her draw her pistol and look around her.

No one. They were alone.

Jacob lay nearby, unmoving. Illary lay further down the slope. Those bastards had kicked her body out of the way while setting up the claymore.

Jana stumbled more than walked over to Jacob. To her profound relief, she found he was still breathing. Knocked out for a while at least, but alive.

She turned and glared at the jungle into which Morel and the others had disappeared.

Two fragmentation grenades remained in Jacob's vest pocket. She took them.

His MP5 and her shotgun had been buried, but Illary's shotgun lay nearby. She took it, topped it up with the last of her shells, and trotted down the slope.

As she got to the bottom, Illary's leg shifted.

Hope leaped in her heart, and she rushed over to check on her Quechua friend.

Yes, she was alive. The bullet had only glanced off her skull, spilling an appalling amount of blood but not killing her.

Not for lack of trying. Jana glared again at the jungle and ran into the bushes, a hunter searching for prey.

Her rage and desire for revenge did not dull her instincts. As soon as she got into the cover of the underbrush, she kept low and looked around her with every step.

The jungle seemed to have gone back to its usual state. Through the ringing that still muffled her hearing, she could hear birds cry. The softer sounds of the jungle, and any creeping footsteps, were lost to her, but she suspected that if the birds had started to call out again, after being silenced by that frightening detonation, they didn't sense any predators lying in wait in the area.

No, if those bandits hadn't set up an ambush at the tunnel opening, that meant they were confident the tunnel would bury her and Jacob.

They would have made a beeline back to camp to grab their provisions. Perhaps they were on their way back to their boat, a day's hike away, in order to grab picks and shovels and start digging out the tunnel again.

The packs were hidden amid the roots of a large tree just to the east of the clearing. Jana made for it.

As she drew closer, she moved with more caution, searching carefully all around her before passing from one bit of cover to the next. Through the ringing in her ears, she heard upraised voices. It sounded like an argument.

She could see the tree up ahead, a thick trunk rising above the underbrush. Getting behind a tree nearby, she peered through the gaps in the foliage.

Only one of them was visible, the guy who had claimed to be a tour operator. Jana couldn't recall his name at the moment. It didn't matter. It had been an alias anyway.

He was obviously arguing with someone to Jana's right, frowning and gesticulating wildly. The buzz in her ears kept her from catching the words. She could guess what was being said. Most of the team had been killed, and the treasure sealed away.

A different voice replied. Morel's. Once again she couldn't catch any words, but it sounded reassuring. Yes, they could excavate the tunnel. No problem. Everyone else who knew about it was dead.

Jana hoped they'd start fighting each other.

The tour operator's anger lessened a bit, and he looked more sulky than confrontational. He moved a little, revealing the other mercenary behind him.

The three were clustered close together. Good.

Jana pulled out one of the grenades. She needed to get closer. This was too far for her to throw. Her arms trembled from fatigue and a dozen minor injuries. She couldn't trust her aim with a grenade at this point. It was a miracle she was even standing.

She pulled the pin, holding onto the lever to keep the timer from starting. Only when she threw it would the lever spring aside, setting off a two-second timer.

As she advanced, she lost sight of the mercenaries. The voices stopped. She picked up speed, and suddenly they appeared, all three turning to stare at her openmouthed. Still too far away.

She burst into a sprint, winding up like a baseball pitcher. The mercenaries spread out, leveling their weapons.

Jana tossed the grenade and threw herself on the ground.

Rolling to the side to get some cover behind a tangle of roots, she pulled out the second grenade just as the first one went off.

She poked her head up and found all three of the men down, but widely spread, probably too widely spread for them all to be dead or seriously injured.

The two guys from the boat were closer together, and moving. Morel was off a bit to the side and not moving. She threw the grenade at the two from the boat. It fell short. Too short?

One didn't seem to see it. The other got halfway up before the grenade blew them both apart.

Jana rose, readying her shotgun. She paced forward, keeping a close eye on Morel. That bastard was full of tricks.

He looked pretty bloody, though. One of his ankles was twisted at an unnatural angle, half torn off by some shrapnel. Three or four lesser wounds marred different parts of his body.

As Jana got within ten feet of him, his eyes snapped open and his hand went for the pistol at his side.

A shotgun blast ended his treacherous life.

Jana stood there, stunned at the bloody havoc she had dealt out to these criminals. The fact that they deserved it only partially eased her conscience.

She checked each one of them, nudging them with her foot to make sure they were well and truly dead, then she circled back to Morel and looked down at him.

He had been a bit like Jacob. A veteran. He probably had some mental scars from whatever he had seen and done in the French Foreign Legion. And then he had joined a law enforcement agency. Physically capable and experienced, he could have been a champion for law and order.

But instead he had turned to the other side for nothing more important than money.

No, she decided, *he wasn't like Jacob at all.*

Jana bent over and pulled the statuette of Supay out of Morel's pocket. A bit of blood was spattered on it. She wiped if off with some leaves and put it in her own pocket.

She hurried over to her pack hidden amid the roots, where she had a first aid kit. Grabbing this, she sprinted back to the site of the tunnel. She hoped she'd still be in time to save Illary and Jacob.

CHAPTER TWENTY FIVE

An hour later, Jana leaned back against a tree, utterly spent. Illary and Jacob lay side by side in the shade, fully bandaged and dosed with painkillers and antibiotics. Even the smallest scratch could go septic in these conditions, and they had a lot more than a small scratch. With a fern she had plucked, she waved away the insects that tried to land on them. She didn't do the same for herself. The pain and weariness were so profound she was past caring.

Illary was breathing regularly. Her pulse seemed OK. While she had lost a lot of blood, she would pull through.

Jacob's wounds were less severe, but he had started this mission depleted. He was unconscious more out of exhaustion than anything else.

At least they were alive. And it seemed none of the other groups remained. That massive explosion and the plume of rock dust it sent into the sky should have brought them running long before now.

They could camp here safely enough, and hopefully Jacob would be sufficiently recovered by morning for them to fashion a stretcher and carry Illary back to the river.

She pulled the statuette of Supay from her pocket and studied it. It was a hideous thing, and yet had a strange attraction beyond its historical value. Modern society tended to avoid thinking about death, except in the abstract through video games and movies. But traditional societies from the Inca to the Tibetans all had gods of death and festivals associated with death. Even her own ancestors, the Germanic and Celtic tribes of Europe, had respected the inevitable fate that all humans faced. To deny it was to be less than a whole person.

What had disgusted her about her father's and Jacob's professions was in fact something that had to be reconciled with life.

They both killed. A lot. And she had killed too. But they had all done it to save life, and none had ever taken life unnecessarily.

She brought the figurine of Supay into a shaft of light peeking through the forest canopy. It played on the gemstones of its eyes and made the golden surface gleam.

This isn't a god of death, it's a god of death AND life. That's why the occultist wanted it. Morel said he wanted to live forever. Well, he's going to be living forever in a prison once I'm through with him.

Jana struggled to her feet and set the statuette between the prone figures of her two friends. She didn't know exactly why she did it, just that it seemed appropriate. Killers who tried to save lives.

Like her. Like what she had become.

She let out a little shiver, but the thought didn't bother her as much as it used to. She had become at peace with it now.

And that made her forgive her father.

He had raised her, protected her, and spent as much time as his unimaginably heavy duties had allowed. And he had saved this good man lying at her feet when everyone else wanted to kill him.

And … had he saved her again? That coded message sent to Jacob's CIA phone. Who else could have sent that? Could Dad really be alive?

Jacob seemed convinced he had died in ISIS territory. Perhaps he was mistaken.

If so, they needed to find out. She'd go to the ends of the earth to find out.

That will be the biggest mission of all, but not the last. I know where the site of El Dorado is. We can come back with a larger team and excavate it. The mercenaries got nothing, and no one else was around to see where the entrance was.

But I have to find out what happened to Dad first.

Suddenly she became aware that she wasn't alone.

She heard no sound, saw no movement, but she became convinced, from one instant to the next, that several sets of eyes rested upon her.

Slowly she raised her hands above her head and turned.

For a moment she saw no one, but then she picked out a dark pair of eyes staring at her from the shadows.

Then she saw another pair, and another.

Figures emerged from the jungle.

They were naked, their bodies painted in various designs of red and black. Most carried bows and arrows, the arrowheads tipped with some sticky resin she felt sure was poison. A few had metal machetes and a couple of them had rifles.

The local tribe. Probably the one the guide for the narcos came from.

I'm dead.

One figure walked ahead of the rest. Jana gasped when she saw what the man carried.

The head of another tribesman. He had it gripped by the hair so it was upright, mouth slack and with hooded eyes half open.

The narcos' guide? She had never gotten a good look at him.

All eyes turned to the figure of Supay standing between Illary and Jacob. The natives went to one knee, bowed their heads, and then stood. Jana didn't move a muscle.

One of the tribesmen stepped forward. He had a machete dangling from a homemade sheath strapped to a factory-manufactured belt.

"*¿Hablas español?*" he asked.

"*Sí.*"

They continued in that language.

"We have killed a traitor to our tribe," he said, gesturing toward the head the other man carried. "He wanted to help outsiders come and steal the old gods."

"You worship Supay and the others?"

"No. Those are the gods of the mountain people, those who live in cold places that always see the sun. They are not our gods. But all gods must be honored, and they are guests in our land."

"The people we killed wanted to steal what's inside that cave."

"And you wouldn't have?"

Jana paused before deciding honesty was the best policy. "Yes, but I wouldn't have killed for it. I came because one of the original archaeologists was a teacher of mine. When he and his crew got killed, we came to seek justice."

"You're not from the Peruvian government?"

"I'm not from any government."

"And him?" the tribesman asked, pointing at Jacob.

"He's from the U.S. government. Some of the archaeologists were U.S. citizens. Illary here is from Interpol. Do you know what that is?"

"I went to school in Lima. I hated it and came back here."

"I see." She hesitated. "What are you going to do with us?"

Instead of answering, he turned to the others and they began to speak in their own language. An older man, the bottom half of his face painted black and the top half painted red, seemed to lead the conversation and others deferred to him. He pointed at the statuette several times. Jana shifted from one foot to the other, nervous. She saw no way she could get away from these people, and even if she could grab her gun, she wouldn't use it.

At last, the translator turned back to her.

"We will let you go. But you must promise never to reveal what you saw here."

"I promise."

She didn't feel good about letting go one of the great archaeological discoveries of the twenty-first century, but if this cave was still an existing place of worship, then she wouldn't interfere with it. It counted as living cultural heritage and not an ancient site.

The translator stared at her for a second, his liquid brown eyes studying her.

"If any outsiders come here looking for the cave," he said, "we will kill them."

"Why didn't you kill the archaeologists?"

"We didn't know they had found it until too late. We had to move our women and children to a new village deeper in the jungle because of all the outsiders searching through the area. The narcos are especially bad to us, and then we discovered that one of our own," he made a contemptuous gesture toward the head, "had sold himself to the narcos. He told us he was only helping big game hunters along the river, people who never ventured too deep into the jungle. We didn't mind that, but when we found out what he was really doing, he was no longer part of our tribe."

Jana gave a concerned look at her companions.

"We can't leave yet. Not until these two are on their feet."

Another discussion in the native language. Several of the warriors peeled off and disappeared into the woods. Jana heard them cutting branches and vines. Within a couple of minutes they came back with several lengths of vine and many small branches. In a flash they expertly tied the vines together, wove the branches between them, padded them with a pile of leaves, and created two stretchers.

Just as they finished, a hunter cried out in their language and came running up to them out of the jungle, holding another statuette. She recognized it as Ayar Cachi, a chaos god who caused earthquakes. The tribesmen gathered together and spoke for a moment, all looking at it.

"Where did he find that?" Jana asked.

"The Peruvian mercenaries, the group you found here and killed, had stashed away their packs. It was in one of them. Come."

With infinite care, aided by Jana, they placed Jacob and Illary onto the stretchers. The chief picked up the figure of Supay and put it in a bag made of the pelt of some jungle creature.

"We will carry your friends to the river where you can get on your boat and leave," the translator said.

"Thank you." Jana hesitated a minute, then got the courage to ask. "Are you going to dig through to the tunnel and return Supay and Ayar Cachi to the room with the other gods?"

"Yes."

"There are a bunch of dead men in there, thieves who wanted to steal the gold. When you clear them out could you put the burned bodies of my friends into the tunnel instead? You'll find them on the fire in their campground, burned by the mercenaries we killed. While they wanted to take the gods, they wanted to take them to study them, not to sell them. And I know their leader, Professor Nasby, would have left the site alone if you had come and explained to him that it was sacred to you. It would have pained him to do so, but he would have done it. He and the others would have wanted to be buried with the gods, to be part of the site."

The translator turned to the others and there was another discussion. When he finished, Jana couldn't help but notice the discussion hadn't lasted as long as the one about whether or not to let her live.

"We will do it," he said.

"Thank you."

They set out. One of the hunters carried her pack. Others carried the rest of the guns and equipment, saying through the translator that all would be returned to her once they reached the river.

Although Jana was exhausted, she did not want to ask to remain in this tribe's territory any longer. It sounded like they had suffered enough from outsiders. She did stop briefly to say a last goodbye to the bodies of her old mentor and his crew before turning away and heading down the path to the river.

As they left the camp behind, Jacob groaned and shifted in his stretcher. Jana moved up to him and held his hand.

His head lolled from side to side, and his eyes fluttered open.

It took him a second to take in the situation.

"What the hell? Have we been taken prisoner?"

"No, everything's all right, Jacob. Morel and the others are dead. Illary is alive. The local tribe who owns this land is taking us to the river."

"They're all right? They're not going to be a problem?"

"Yes, Jacob." She squeeze his hand. "We're safe."

"I'm sorry we didn't find the crew alive."

Jana hung her head. "They were dead before we even left Mexico City."

He squeezed her hand. "Sorry. At least they got to see that room. We did too."

The sparkle in his eyes showed he had been in just as much awe as she had. She remembered how when she had been going through all the great archaeological discoveries she had made in the past few months, only the first and the least important—the Roman mosaic in Morocco—had been made alone.

All others had been with him.

She bent down and kissed him on the forehead.

"Thank you," she said.

"Maybe you can thank me more when we aren't surrounded by a bunch of naked dudes with poison arrows."

Jana laughed. "You're such a moron."

Jacob put a hand on his heart. "At your service, madam."

Jana thought for a moment as she continued walking down the path holding his hand.

"Would you do something for me, Jacob?"

"Anything. To say I owe you is the understatement of the century."

"That message you got ... do you think it could be from my dad?"

"I don't know. I mean, it can't be. But ... I've seen an awful lot of things in my life that can't be."

Jana nodded. "So have I."

"You want me to help you find him?"

"Yeah."

"Then the answer is yes. I'll do whatever it takes to bring Aaron Peters back to you. I stole him from you without ever realizing I was stealing him from you. I'm sorry about that."

"No, I was overreacting. He was helping you. You needed it."

"I'm still sorry. And to repay my debt to him, and you, we'll find out who really sent that message."

"Together?" Jana asked.

"Damn right, together. Who can stop us?"

Jana smiled down at him. "No one can."

They continued down the path, holding hands and heading for the river that would take them to their next adventure together.

EPILOGUE

The Pamir Mountains, northeast Afghanistan near the Tajikistan border
That same day ...

Agent 313, known in his old life as Aaron Peters, sat on the dirt floor with his back resting on the plastered stone wall. The room was dark except for a bit of light filtering through the rickety old shutters and peeking under the bottom of the door that led to the rest of the simple peasant's dwelling in which he was imprisoned.

He could kick down that door easily enough, or pry off the rusty bars just outside the shutters, but he'd never make it out of here. His original captor had soon been joined by a team of others, and kept a close watch on the door, the window, and the entire perimeter.

And these weren't Taliban fighters, or men from one of the tribal or warlord militias. They might have posed as such, they might have gotten their initial experience with those groups, but they had risen to a far more elite fighting force.

The Order.

Aaron had been hunting the Order for a long time now, ever since he had staggered, bleeding and only half alive, out of Raqqa all those years ago.

He had been declared dead after that mission, both officially and in the eyes of his fellow agents. Jacob Snow had filed the after-action report, and the younger man was convinced his mentor had died in the blast that took out the ISIS arms depot. Most of those who had read the report agreed with Jacob's assessment. There was no way Aaron Peters could have survived.

And yet he had, and the higher echelons of the CIA had seen his supposed death as an opportunity.

They put out a fake conversation on some channels they knew were insecure announcing his death and playing through a false debate about whether or not to lie about his still being alive. After a few weeks of this, they made an official announcement of his death. Now the bad

150

guys were convinced he was dead far more than if they had simply read a death notice.

Aaron disappeared for a while, both to heal and to train. Once ready, he began hunting the Order wherever it appeared—in Thailand, in Mali, in Turkmenistan, and eventually Afghanistan.

Aaron stood and paced back and forth in the small room as much as his leg chains would allow. He didn't have much time. They'd kept him here for a few days now, waiting for something. A secure pick-up to remove him to a more secure location? Probably. They'd want to interrogate him at their leisure, and with the best medical assistance possible.

They knew he wouldn't break to physical torture. Only mind-altering truth drugs might make him slip up and say something.

And the Order had the best interrogation drugs in the world.

There was no escape from these people, and no compromising. He was doomed.

But not Jana. He held that last and greatest victory close to his heart. With a compact yet highly powerful satellite phone hidden in the sole of his shoe, he had texted Jacob's secure phone using their personal code. It had been a terrible breach of security protocol to reveal that he was alive, but his daughter's life was on the line and he didn't feel the least bit guilty.

The phone was hidden back in his boot, its battery drained. It had had only enough juice for one brief message.

That was all he needed. The Order had originally captured him by revealing that Jana had been kidnapped and that they knew his real identity. They had done their job well, finding out first that he was alive and that he was the elusive Agent 313. Then they had tracked down his daughter.

But they hadn't used that threat since. No proof of life, no photos, no voice message. Nothing. They had her and then they lost her. Jacob had done his job. He hoped the younger man had taken out a bunch of Order operatives in the rescue mission.

He hoped he had gotten Jana out unharmed.

Aaron Peters did some burpees and jumping jacks to keep himself fit. He'd been a POW before, and that situation was a constant struggle against despair and apathy. The only way to win was to keep active, even if you were stuck in an eight-by-ten room with no furniture other than a pot to piss in.

As he exercised, he ran through the possible reasons they had captured him. The Order wanted him out of the way, obviously, but it was more than that. They'd found his only weakness and exploited it, hoping he'd talk.

But talk about what? His knowledge of CIA covert ops was limited to Afghanistan, Pakistan, and the frontier with Iran. And they knew all that would get switched around after he vanished and was presumed captured. His intel value was limited.

Unless it was old intel they were after. He'd been on a lot of missions all over the world, and the Order had its tentacles everywhere. What if they wanted insight into the illegal uranium shipments from South Africa? Or the weapon systems being developed by Brazil? Or details of the opium trade in the Far East?

He could tell them all about these things and so much more.

Yeah, it was probably something like that. Actually, they probably wanted every bit of intel they could scrape out of his brains with those drugs of theirs. A couple of years back, he raided an Order base in Kurdistan to extract an agent who had gone through Order interrogation. There wasn't much left of the man, just a delirious, babbling mess that would never be an intelligent adult again.

A tremor in his chest. For a moment, Aaron Peters didn't know what it was. Then he recognized it.

Fear. Not fear of death, like he had felt for most days of the past twenty years, but a deeper fear. A fear of losing one's mind.

They'll do that to me, Aaron thought. *They'll do it for sure.*

He decided then and there that no matter what the odds, he'd make a break for it. He'd rather die than get turned into a vegetable.

And he'd rather die than give the Order anything to increase its power.

For so long, the Order's motives had eluded the secret services of the world. It would shore up a democracy one month, then lead a coup the next. It would take out an entire terrorist cell, only to fund a different one. Only years of careful study, and figuring out when the secretive group was actually behind an event, did a pattern emerge.

Chaos. They wanted to sow chaos. They were building up a network of mutually hostile forces to a breaking point of tension, and when the dam burst and a flood of violence swept the world, then the Order would step in and take control.

Not direct control. They were too smart to fall for the lure of nationhood like ISIS had done. It made them easier to bomb. No, the

152

Order didn't work like that. They would move into key positions of power in international arms and drug production and smuggling, and with the chaos they had themselves unleashed making boom times for their new businesses, they would rake in the profits.

And those profits would fund control in the corridors of power in every important nation in the world.

And once they had that, world domination was an achievable goal.

They had the organization, they had the personnel, all they needed were the opportunity and the funding.

So no, Aaron Peters would not let his gold mine of secret information fall into the Order's hands. He'd die first.

All he needed was an opportunity.

He finished his exercise routine, the thin film of sweat on his skin feeling cool in the mountain cabin, his breath refreshingly deep and fast. He took to pacing again.

As he did, his mind cast back to his daughter, Jana, and his adopted son, Jacob. Those two had never really known each other. He wondered, now that Jacob had hopefully rescued Jana alive, how they were getting along. He hoped they teamed up. They'd do well together.

They'd need to. Because even if the Order got nothing from him, he could tell their plans were far more advanced than he realized. Pretty soon they'd be unleashing a wave of violence and disruption that would make World War Two look like a playground fistfight.

Bad times were coming. Very bad.

And he had no idea if the CIA and all its allies were strong enough to stop it.

NOW AVAILABLE!

TARGET FIVE
(The Spy Game—Book #5)

"Thriller writing at its best... A gripping story that's hard to put down."
--Midwest Book Review, Diane Donovan (re Any Means Necessary)

"One of the best thrillers I have read this year. The plot is intelligent and will keep you hooked from the beginning. The author did a superb job creating a set of characters who are fully developed and very much enjoyable. I can hardly wait for the sequel."
--Books and Movie Reviews, Roberto Mattos (re Any Means Necessary)

From #1 bestselling and USA Today bestselling author Jack Mars, author of the critically acclaimed *Luke Stone* and *Agent Zero* series (with over 5,000 five-star reviews), comes an explosive new action-packed espionage series that takes readers on a wild ride across Europe, America, and the world.

A CIA agent, posing as an archeologist in Pakistan, is arrested, and world security hinges on what he knows—and what he found. Jacob Snow, elite soldier-turned-CIA agent, with his mysterious archeologist partner, must race against time to find him, and to free him, before it's too late.

But at every turn the mystery deepens—and time is running out.

An unputdownable action thriller with heart-pounding suspense and unforeseen twists, TARGET FIVE is the fifth novel in an exhilarating new series by a #1 bestselling author that will make you fall in love with a brand-new action hero—and keep you turning pages late into the night. Perfect for fans of Dan Brown, Daniel Silva and Jack Carr.

TARGET SIX is now also available.

Jack Mars

Jack Mars is the USA Today bestselling author of the LUKE STONE thriller series, which includes seven books. He is also the author of the new FORGING OF LUKE STONE prequel series, comprising six books; of the AGENT ZERO spy thriller series, comprising twelve books; of the TROY STARK thriller series, comprising five books; and of the SPY GAME thriller series, comprising six books.

Jack loves to hear from you, so please feel free to visit www.Jackmarsauthor.com to join the email list, receive a free book, receive free giveaways, connect on Facebook and Twitter, and stay in touch!

BOOKS BY JACK MARS

THE SPY GAME
TARGET ONE (Book #1)
TARGET TWO (Book #2)
TARGET THREE (Book #3)
TARGET FOUR (Book #4)
TARGET FIVE (Book #5)
TARGET SIX (Book #6)

TROY STARK THRILLER SERIES
ROGUE FORCE (Book #1)
ROGUE COMMAND (Book #2)
ROGUE TARGET (Book #3)
ROGUE MISSION (Book #4)
ROGUE SHOT (Book #5)

LUKE STONE THRILLER SERIES
ANY MEANS NECESSARY (Book #1)
OATH OF OFFICE (Book #2)
SITUATION ROOM (Book #3)
OPPOSE ANY FOE (Book #4)
PRESIDENT ELECT (Book #5)
OUR SACRED HONOR (Book #6)
HOUSE DIVIDED (Book #7)

FORGING OF LUKE STONE PREQUEL SERIES
PRIMARY TARGET (Book #1)
PRIMARY COMMAND (Book #2)
PRIMARY THREAT (Book #3)
PRIMARY GLORY (Book #4)
PRIMARY VALOR (Book #5)
PRIMARY DUTY (Book #6)

AN AGENT ZERO SPY THRILLER SERIES
AGENT ZERO (Book #1)
TARGET ZERO (Book #2)
HUNTING ZERO (Book #3)
TRAPPING ZERO (Book #4)

Made in United States
Troutdale, OR
09/28/2023

13241406R00099